SWAY POLE

SWAYPOLE

A novel by

Daniel Isaac Morris

VICOA.COM
Pennsylvania, USA

ISBN-10 0-9828250-9-9
ISBN -978-0-9828250-9-9
Published by Vicoa.com

For the Morris, Rogers, Lambert and Kincaid Families.

Thanks to: Don Knotts, Bob Denver, Soupy Sales, Grady Tripp, Mountain Dancer Jesco White and their kin—just for being West Virginians.

For Barbara, Danny, Kelley
Webster and the late Ben Bird

This book is a work of fiction, and any similarities to places or persons, living or dead, is coincidental. While I refer to certain historical facts, be aware that these may at times be fictionalized and intentionally inconsistent with true historical accounts.

There is a bunker designed for the protection and preservation of the Government of The United States of America that was hidden under the Greenbrier Hotel in Lewisburg, West Virginia
http://www.greenbrier.com/site/bunker.aspx

The FBI's Criminal Justice Information Services Division in Clarksburg, West Virginia that is responsible for locating and identifying individuals.
http://www.fas.org/irp/agency/doj/fbi/is/ncic.htm

The IRS Enterprise Computing Center, Martinsville, WV provides information on individuals, businesses and financial institutions.
http://www.irs.gov/efile/article/0,,id=102313,00.html

The National Radio Astronomy Observatory, Greenbank, WV operates the world's largest fully steerable single aperture antenna along with several other radio telescopes.
http://www.gb.nrao.edu/

Arthurdale, WV is a New Deal communal village that was built during the Franklin D. Roosevelt administration. It was taken on as a personal project by FDR's wife Eleanor and is still referred to as "Her Little Village." Partly restored and partly a ruin, it struggles for existence today.
http://www.arthurdaleheritage.org/

This is also the realm of feuds, the largest armed insurrection since the Civil War, monsters, ghosts, alien creatures, mothmen, men in black, dark dwarfs, snake handlers, a government sponsored commune, cannibal hill-billies—but then, the reader should decide what's real and what's fiction.

Prologue

There was nothing intrinsically sinister about the region, just as there didn't appear to be anything particularly threatening about the stream running through it. It may be the shadowland of the deep valley that made it seem unsettling. Perhaps it was the fog that settled and rose from the stream that caused an ominous ambiance that seemed bereft of sounds of life — sounds that appeared to be absorbed by the flow of water rushing toward where it hadn't been before. For some, the valley was a quiet restful retreat, for others, it was an unearthly realm with all of the cheery charm of a cemetery plot at dusk.

The name Ruby certainly had nothing to do with the gemstone, but it might have been the result of some early, romantic settler's lost love. Tall tales abound, but no one remembers exactly how Ruby County and its stream, Ruby Branch, were named. It wasn't much more than a creek running into the Shenandoah. But eons ago it was as if some prehistoric Paul Bunyan cut a furrow deep into the rock-strewn hills lying on either side, a gash that allowed Ruby Branch's waters to run cold and deep from a source high in the misty Blue Ridge.

The Ruby was deceptive, seemingly inviting and refreshing. When summers were hot, the waters below the steep banks of the stream gurgled and babbled a beckoning call, but few would dare enter the rushing stream to defy the numbing cold or the depths of its waters.

The river's siren call was especially strong one searing summer day when two boys, barely teenagers, walked the steep embankments of the Ruby Branch much as a tightrope walker would tempt the open space far below.

Summer insects angrily protested the heat and humidity of that steamy afternoon as one of the boys mounted a retaining wall above the raging stream. In his imagination he was high above the carnival midway crowd, above his companion who must be looking up at him in admiration. The walker, in the hope of getting a reaction from the other boy, feigned losing his balance, pretending to stumble, but deftly escaping certain death by regaining his feet. The expected response didn't come from his companion, so he attempted to move on.

Like Karl Wallenda's waltz on the wire, the boy's walk on the wall ended abruptly. The Ruby Branch continued, now carrying the lifeless body of a young boy in its relentless current, a current that had worn away layers of the past—and the present.

Chapter 1

Ramón Villavicencio came to America long before *Batalla de Yaguajay*. Those were the days when el *Jefe* was a lawyer for the poor. Of course, this was long before Cubans floated on inner tubes to Florida. It was before Fidel, *El Barbudo*, would strut the world stage.

Ramón traveled from Matanzas to *Tierra de la Promesa* by "legal means," which is to say he stole enough money to pay the right people for the correct papers. Unlike many immigrants in those days, he was unskilled, uneducated, and relatively ignorant of how things were done in his new home country, let alone *Tierra de la Promesa*. He arrived in Miami and found a squalid place to dwell in what would become Little Havana.

After several poor attempts at panhandling, he pondered his lot in life. After what socio-types would have called a "skills assessment," he decided the only thing he might be able to do was to become an actor. He reached this life-changing conclusion because he had always liked the movies.

Certainly a naïve decision, but one he could never change, one of those beyond-recall moves with which he would be stuck for life. So Ramón left the relative comfort of the known to strike out for the unknown, the magical, legendary Hollywood, *Tierra de Sueños*. One skill he might have listed was an uncanny ability to find free transportation.

Of course, Ramón knew nothing of being cool—he swiped his shades in a convenience store—and nothing of the structure of Hollywood, the land of who-you-know. Eventually, he found himself in a world he knew. He knew it in Cuba, knew it in Little Havana, and he came to know it in Southern California. He knew a life of the street, subsistence, washing dishes, cleaning pools, mowing lawns, and any daywork when he needed money. When he couldn't find work, he rummaged in trash bins and stole things that weren't fastened down.

No one will ever know how Ramón happened to be near the intersection of West Sunset and South Carmelina Avenue that afternoon, nor what drew him to a trash bin there. It's reasonable to assume Ramón was going about his daily activities, going through whatever trash he encountered. It's equally reasonable to assume he sought this area of Brentwood because the trash was sure to include things that would be trash to the rich and famous, but treasure to just about anyone else.

Brentwood was a place of gates, big dogs, and security guards, so he couldn't stay long. Among the garbage treasures, Ramón found a brown shopping bag stuffed with things hastily thrown out. Perhaps these are the belongings of a rich filmmaker who has been thrown out by his beautiful actress wife, Ramón fantasized.

Once out of sight, he would sort through the bag and throw out worthless items, but his immediate intent was to get back to familiar territory. For him, familiar territory was a culvert that ran under a road in one of the nearby parks. He called it Culvert City and found that people thought he meant Culver

City, so he used it as a home address.

Inside the bag were letters, a partially melted waxy thing, papers, empty pill bottles, beer cans, and a book. Ramón opened the book and found that there was some type, but the story was written in longhand. Some of the writing was completely blacked out, but that was no matter to Ramón, because he couldn't read it anyway. He flipped some pages to see if there were any pictures, but there were only empty pages toward the back.

He was about to toss the book into the small stream below his culvert home when it occurred to him it might be a movie script and the plain paper might be handy since toilet paper wasn't always available and the book was a good place to keep any pictures he might find. So, as luck would have it, Ramón Villavicencio kept the bag and put the book inside with a few of his other meager possessions.

No one is sure how it happened, and no one would ever believe the rags-to-riches story his press agent would eventually spin. Only one part of the story is believable, the part where he was "discovered" near his culvert home.

As the tale is told, an assistant casting director looking for some bums—later known as "homeless people—" to inhabit a film, happened upon Ramón, offered him scale for a day's work, and the rest of the story is the stuff press agents are paid to produce.

One Hollywood investigative reporter claims Ramón's fame came about because of his relationship with a major studio head. That tale may be true, because as the story goes, Ramón was caught in bed with the executive by a private investigator. And, it turned out the studio head was really a head, cocaine, just like everyone else.

Soon Ramón Villavicencio had an agent and came to be known as Ramón de Varo because his agent said it made people think of Ramón Navarro. He believed the world was ready for a new Latin lover.

Ramón never did learn to read, and he had to learn the scripts as well as English pronunciations phonetically, by rote, with the assistance of well-paid coaches who were sworn to secrecy. He went on to appear in short supporting roles until he got his big break. Sadly, his big chance was a starring role in a picture that made *Plan Nine from Outer Space* look like high art. The thing was so bad it never achieved cult-film status.

Ramón appeared now and then in small roles. He tried out for the role of Emmanuel in the film version of Terry Southern's *Candy*. Of course, he was passed over for an actor with far more talent and substance—Ringo Starr. He did get a similar role as a Mexican gardener in a porn movie made in Mexico, but his chances for stardom were about as likely as a scene in which John Wayne kisses Gabby Hayes. He appeared as a pony handler in a film by the same producer, but it was his last appearance in a film.

As with most rising Hollywood stars, Ramón de Varo fell victim to sex, drugs, and alcohol, a Tinsel Town trip for de Varo that took Ramón Villavicencio along with him. He became terrified by paranoia and told whoever would listen that the *Policía Nacional Revolucionaria* was after him, or sometimes the CIA, FBI, or the Mafia. Again he took up residence in his former Culvert City home, but not for long. The glamorous Hollywood life required a toll be paid.

Before coming to America, Ramón met his Cousin Leon. Leon was much younger and had a job. He had told Ramón about the land to the north, the land of the Yankees. He told him of the *béisbol* and the ciné. He would go to America when

14

he had saved enough money, he said.

When Leon arrived in America, he learned quickly that his Hispanic name was a liability, so he decided to become Italian, perhaps Sicilian. So, Leon Villavicencio became Leon Riluttante, a name he picked out of phonebook. Federico Riluttante was a successful attorney, so Leon reckoned the name must be one valued in America.

It may have been a newspaper story about the death of a Hollywood never-was, a where-are-they-now article, or maybe it was a short death notice, or any number of other things that caused Leon to notice one of his many cousins had passed away. He undoubtedly noticed because Villavicencio, at that time, wasn't a common name. In any event, Leon made a formal inquiry about the death of his Cousin Ramón and discovered that he was Ramón's sole heir.

Leon's inheritance wasn't much—a bill for his cousin's cremation and some clothing that should have been burned along with Ramón. Included was a worn brown paper shopping bag containing a rosary, a picture of the Villavicencio family under one of those long sweeping palms, some letters and, unfortunately, a small dog-eared book.

Chapter 2

Crowcroft family's home county in Virginia clung to West Virginia's southern border. It was as if it were an abandoned member of the Virginia Volunteers raising a feeble hand to grasp the renegade part of the Old South that would escape to become a Yankee state during the Civil War. It was here, in the small village of Dillweed that Calais Antonius Crowcroft was born.

The Crowcrofts weren't dirt poor, but they weren't landed gentry either. Caprarius Antonius Crowcroft wasn't exactly sure of his son's lineage, but gave him the traditional Roman family name and accepted him as his own, although he harbored deep suspicions about the town's Methodist minister. It wouldn't be until the kid left home that the son learned his father's name—which translates to "goat"—was well deserved; it was just another family secret.

Calais' nickname was Calley, and his father's was Tony. If things had been different, they would have been known as Big Tony and Little Calley. However, things were quite different. One reason he got stuck with the moniker was his old man's love for gladiator movies and lord knows what other sort of gladiatorial goings-on. Calley had seen magazines in the back of his father's dresser drawer with its pictures of oiled, muscular men that sort of looked like gladiators, but he had better sense than to investigate further. Much later, he would conclude that the old man preferred both genders, but for now he had a standoffish understanding with the old man. They didn't say much to each other, and both liked it that way.

The only time Calley could recall his dad showing any interest in him and his brother was a day when they had gone to town. They stopped at a dollar store and his father bought both kids shiny red whistles. They were plastic, the kind with a ball inside to make them warble.

"Just like the refs use at the basketball court," the old man said as he handed one to each of them. "You blow on these when you're in trouble, and your dad will come running."

Intuitively, Calley knew the old man was blowing smoke, and he knew they would never be the typical Big Guy Dad and Little Guy Son of Southern tradition. Calley seemed to be the only one who noticed the old man was, as usual, full of it.

Calais didn't like his name much, so he told everyone he met they could just call him Calley. He wouldn't have presumed to change his surname, because where he came from, changing one's family name was a major sin, right up there with loving opera, hating NASCAR, and drinking Blue Ribbon from anything but longnecks.

Had he been blessed with a strong woman for a mother, he might have been "her little boy" and grown up with some of his father's predilections. However, his mother wasn't the strong-willed white trash stereotype his father might have taken up with. She came from more genteel Southern stock, and to her mind was simply a victim of a poor choice of mate, marrying beneath her. And nearly everyone agreed.

Priscilla Carter Crowcroft was a typical Southern belle of the ding-a-ling variety. Her father thought Tony was the best catch his low-wattage daughter would ever get. She was forever gullible, naïve, and willing to listen to any yarn her husband or offspring might spin to explain their latest transgression.

So Calley's childhood was simple, permissive, and short. His father ignored him, his mother forgave him, and he ran wild from the time he was a tot until he was a teenager.

His relationship with his brother, Gaius Brutus Crowcroft, or Guy, as he preferred to be called, was as dysfunctional as those he enjoyed with the rest of the family. "The boys never seem to get a long," was his mother's frequent comment. When they weren't in a true knock-down-drag-out, they were constantly quarreling.

Perhaps the name Brutus fit brother Guy too well. If he had grown to adulthood, he would have made a dandy psychopathic serial killer. His early childhood was a profiler's handbook on how to become one. Beginning life with his brutal, kinky father and permissive mother, he took early delight in torturing and killing small animals. This animal cruelty probably began when Tony heaped praise upon his son at the family dinner table for his eagerness in doing away with the old family dog.

This procedure wasn't just putting old Rover to sleep; it took six shots from a .22 rifle.

After that, it seemed Guy took great satisfaction in inflicting pain on any available creature, most of all Calley. Had Guy lived beyond thirteen, Calley most likely would have been the first victim in a long line of serial killings.

Guy was a consistent school bully, and Calley was the constant target of the ire Guy generated among his classmates.

Maybe it would have been better if the older brother had died of some childhood illness, a ruptured appendix, pneumonia, or other natural cause. It might have caused Calley to have a different self-image and outlook on life. But it's doubtful that anything would have changed inside him. He profoundly wished his brother dead, and whether it was by his hand or not, it would have mattered little. He would always see himself as the instrument of his brother's demise.

It wasn't as if Calley was haunted by his brother's untimely death either; that might have been due to his being as vindictive as his sibling. It was just something he had done, and to his mind a necessary part of growing older. His brother's death was dismissed and sent off to the lesser regions of his brain, like a dusty book on the farthest library shelf.

Swimming had never been a Crowcroft strong suit, but Guy fancied himself an excellent swimmer. He was really a three on a ten-scale, but that didn't keep him out of deep water. Calley, on the other hand, didn't believe he could stay above water for more than a few strokes. He managed short distances by keeping his face down and dogpaddling. From time to time, he would surface for air, but as soon has he had a gulp, it was back to his facedown dogpaddle.

Given their swimming skills, they shouldn't have been near the river in the first place. What happened was spur-of-the-moment, one of those irretrievable instants when one fraction of a turn of the wheel and one millisecond of timing could have made all the difference, but it would be a moment impossible to relive for a different outcome. It was a decision that left one of the boys' bloated bodies floating downstream two days later.

Guy, always the daredevil, hopped on a low stone wall built to protect passersby from falling over a ten-foot embankment and into the river below. The wall was at least a foot thick, but the top was too rough for a careless teen to walk. Guy kept his balance for several feet, then stumbled, waved his arms propel-ler-fashion to regain balance, and continued as he reached out to steady himself on his brother's shoulder.

That was when Calley reacted. Without so much as a thought, he reached out and gave Guy a quick, thoughtless push and Guy pitched headlong into the river.

Neither of them realized how cold the water was compared to the hot summer air on the bank. Cramping started almost immediately. And from the time he hit the water, he called to Calley for help—help that didn't come.

"I'm ain't shittin' you," he screamed, "I can't move, I can't swim!"

Somehow Guy had managed to find his red whistle and put it in his mouth. He managed one whimper of a toot, then bubbles.

Blow it out your ass, thought Calley. Always one to recog-nize an opportunity, he sat on the riverbank to wait and watch.

The years passed. Folks said Calley was troubled be-cause his brother accidentally drowned in front of him and he couldn't save him. If anyone had darker thoughts on the subject, they were never mentioned. Calley spent the next four years getting through high school and funding his penchant for fun with petty crime interspersed with random acts of vandal-ism.

"He's a good boy," said Priscilla, "He's just got burdens to bear. It ain't his fault."

When he stole Reverend Paternoster's car and crashed it into the county Veteran's Memorial, the judge didn't quite agree with Calley's mother. His father and the judge convinced him that joining the Navy would be much better than staying around the house and having the old man kick his butt on a

daily basis. The Navy would only be his first escape from the distress of Dilweed.

Chapter 3

The passengers had been on the damned bus for nearly two days as it crossed the Midwest and onto the two-lane blacktops of Ohio, meandering its way toward the Mountain State, a.k.a. West Virginia. After all those tedious flatland interstate miles, anyone would believe the world was as flat as a Waffle House grill. Pennsylvania was never intended to be a destination, but then the driver's mother never intended to raise a meathead either. He managed to get lost more than a few times in West Virginia, and instead of turning southeast, he drove northwest into Pennsylvania, headed for Pittsburgh.

No one was sure if it was a legitimate bus line, and the driver wasn't about to admit to its jitney status. His boss, the bus owner, wanted riders to think it was an official 'Graydog' ship of the line. Bruester Maas chose the name carefully so an inattentive rider would think it was at least a puppy of the well-known bus company. The canine he had painted on the side might have passed a cursory inspection. Bruester insisted it was a Whippet, but except for the ears and color it more re-sembled a Redbone Coonhound than the well-known bus logo he was aiming for.

The driver didn't follow a regular route, but sort of cruised from place to place, picking up the hopeless and hapless for whatever fare he could negotiate. He often whipped into a regular stop in hope of luring unsuspecting travelers aboard. As his passengers boarded, driver Luther Ardavice Simms insisted they call him Lukey. He thought Lukey sounded friendlier and had more Southern charm.

Lukey, whose age and I.Q. converged at around 35, had insisted on finding a shortcut from Cambridge, Ohio to New Martinsville, West Virginia. Things weren't going badly until he lost his way and ended up on some back road with skimpy guardrails that turned into an anaconda, twisting and dropping its way toward the Ohio River. Unfortunately for the just-lunched group, the snaking road flipped back on itself and twisted into a sheepshank knot. The passengers might have protested had there been more than just the five of them.

One of the group sat in the middle. Calais Antonius Crow-croft was fresh out of the Navy and headed for home in Dill-weed, Virginia. Three years of typing duty rosters as a yeo-man stationed in Nevada convinced him that the seafaring life wasn't for him. So, he took an early out and headed for home to whatever awaited. His Navy discharge and what he might do afterward were as unplanned as the early years of his young life.

While in the service of his country, the Navy kept him in shape so he was more muscular than average. His close-cropped light brown hair and tanned skin revealed his Euro-pean heritage and his recent military discharge. But the dead giveaway was his shoes: spit-shined, black military oxfords that civilians living near a naval base looked for if they suspected someone was mingling with their herd. Excepting the oxfords, he looked like any college student, wearing a typical uniform of jeans and a ragged sweatshirt with the sleeves cut off. Unlike most collegians, his belt buckle was much too large with too much metal to be cool. The best description perhaps was a preppie bubba.

Like all of the other passengers, Calley carried his share of baggage, not all of it stowed in his duffle bag.

Chapter 4

Devnet Keavy was destined for trouble the day she was born—or that's how she saw it anyway. Stuck between adolescence and adulthood, it seemed she would never escape her teen years tribulations. Her mother died when she was eighteen months old, and her father cared for her as best he could. When she was eleven, her Aunt Sis moved in to care for "Little Devey" and her dad. Devey took an instant dislike to Aunt Sis.

Siobhan Keavy was nearly seventy and had the countenance of someone who constantly smelled something foul. To Devey, Aunt Sis was a jailer, not a caregiver. She seldom smiled and Devey couldn't recall ever seeing her laugh. She was the archetypical Aunt Sourpuss, hair worn in the style of a fundamentalist Bible-thumper, she never cursed, "shoot" being the extent of her epithetical vocabulary.

Aunt Sis considered it her calling to keep Devey's daddy from showing his little girl any affection, for fear it would arouse "evil feelings and impure thoughts." Siobhan Keavy considered it among her solemn duties to keep Devey from sex, drugs, rock and roll, and any other diversion or entertainment.

Devey's sole companion, other than Aunt Sis, was Missy Anne, a conglomeration of rags, yarn, and thread that Devey assembled from whatever scraps came her way. Missy Anne had gained and lost parts of her body over the years and was unrecognizable to anyone but Devey. She had the distinct feeling Aunt Sis was determined that her charge would follow in her footsteps to become as she had, a dried-up old maid.

Trouble began the moment Aunt Sis stepped through the door to announce her arrival to save them all from a life of loneliness, potential sin, and eternal hellfire. Devey's first thoughts of causing Aunt Sis problems came later, taking root during her early teens. The rebellious teenage years are tough enough for any parent, but Aunt Sis saw them as an affront to her basic dignity and Christian values. Her assignment was, she said, "her cross to bear."

For a couple of years, Devey had been forming plans to mitigate the old biddy's influence. Her thoughts were initially benign, hiding her reading glasses or placing a "lost" darning needle strategically in her chair. But as time progressed, her thoughts turned darker.

At first, she just planned ways to get rid of the annoying aunt, but her plans never got off the ground. Sis would never be persuaded to leave; after all, she had nowhere to go. So for long periods, the girl gave up on ever being free of the "witch," as Devey now thought of her.

Devey couldn't abide the sight of blood and never thought of herself as violent or a murderer. She wished many times that Sis were a kin of the Wicked Witch in the *Wizard of Oz*. If that were so, she could simply spray water on Sis, who would puddle into oblivion. Such was the extent of Devey's premeditated murderous thoughts, until she neared adulthood, when her thoughts became an obsession.

The relentless Aunt Sis still thought of her niece as "Little Devey," who had to be protected and sheltered from a future in the fires of Hades. Now an adult and nearly twenty-one, Devnet Keavy once again began to think of eliminating her jailer once and for all. As with many of that age, it didn't occur to her that she could pick up and leave at any time she chose.

Aunt Sis never seemed to age. She was old when she arrived and Devey was a child, and years later, she seemed just as old. Any hope of Sis dying from a malignancy or just old age was remote. Sickness and death were reserved, it seemed, for good people, while witches endured for years. Anyhow, there never seemed to be any young witches.

All of that changed one day when Devey's aunt complained of chest pains. She took chamomile, flaxseed, baking soda, aspirin, Goody Powders, and an Epsom salts laxative, but nothing seemed to offer relief.

After a few days of this, Devey's dad suggested she see a doctor. After a few more days, he demanded that she see Dr. Vinny, down in Logan. Sis moaned that she would never return. They would take her to the hospital for tests, poke and probe her, operate, then send her to a rest home to die. Devey's hopes soared.

As it turned out, there were tests, scans, poking, and probing, and finally a diagnosis and prescriptions. But eventually they sent her home, much to Devey's disappointment, not to die, but to recuperate. Devey's short-lived hope for Aunt Sis's quick demise was dashed. Now Aunt Sis had blood pressure pills and heart pills, stuff that Devey reckoned would let her live forever.

"Lisinopril, Simvastatin, and aspirin," she announced to Devey as she hit the door. "Got these here vitamins too." She held up a bottle of capsules.

"Cheap generic versions of the real overpriced stuff," said Devey's father. "Good thing, too. Can't afford much with Medicare. Aspirin's cheap, though. About all I ever take. Wonder drug, vitamins are horse puckey." He took the yellow bottle of seemingly yellow capsules, held it up to the light, and grimaced.

Chapter 5

At first the driver thought it was a mirage. It must have been one of those undulating, heat-generated apparitions that appear in film sequences shot with long focal length lenses. That was it, he thought, a *Raising Arizona*—Biker from Hell out there on the tarmac hanging out, shotgun in hand, waiting for an innocent victim.

Of course, it was nothing of the sort. A past-middle-aged woman stood by the roadside, hand waving feebly to flag down the approaching coach. Beside her stood a younger woman, who looked to be a little more than eighteen.

Normally, Lukey would have blown by them. But economic good sense overrode the need for speed. Lukey applied what brakes survived from the last reline job, and they screeched to a stop.

A dozing Calley was jerked into the here-and-now by the sudden inertia of the halt and the hissing air and screaming brakes. Lukey threw the door open with a whip of his wrist.

"Where ya'll goin'?" he asked.

"We was trying to get to down around Madison, down in Boone County," replied the older woman.

"Ain't going off onto any other routes. I'm going to head down the other interstate when I get to Charleston. But you're welcome to ride along that far if you like."

"I suppose we can hitch from Charleston on down. How much?"

"How much? Oh, the fare ..." Lukey sized up the pair, guessing how much cash they were likely to part with. Too high, he might lose the fare. Too low, hauling their dead butts to Charleston wouldn't be worth the diesel fuel. In desperation, he looked at Calley, who shrugged.

He pretended to refer to papers on a scroungy clipboard hanging beside his seat. "The fare from here is exactly $17.39."

"That for both of us, or apiece?"

"Apiece, of course," he responded confidently. "I'll tell you what. So I don't have to make change, I'll let you both on for $34 even. How's that?"

"More than it's worth, but I reckons how we don't have much choice." She searched through a ragged homemade purse. She dug out some dollar bills, gum wrappers, a WalMart receipt, and a rubber band. Then like a carnival magician dipping into a gaffed egg bag, she produced from the depths of the purse three crisp tens and added four ragged ones that would never see the inside of a change making machine again.

Lukey pocketed the cash. "Have a seat." He noticed the older woman took the seat vacated by the female of a couple who had recently departed. And the younger woman took the seat a man had occupied across the aisle.

Sitting in a seat close to the front of the bus, Calley observed the younger woman. Not really thin, she just looked it. She had adequate breasts and a figure to go with them. In fact, her figure was a whole lot more than adequate, under baggy jeans, plain T-shirt, and cardigan. Her hair wasn't the Nordic blonde typical of bleached beach girls. She had the honey-colored hair and blue eyes typical of the Celtic heritage of Appalachia, a mixture of Scots and Irish. Faith Hill and Shania Twain looked like Gladys Ormphby by comparison. She had put on a pair of horned-rim reading glasses as she settled in with a book. They gave her such an intelligent look that she made everyone else on the bus look dimwitted. Actually this was not all that difficult.

Calley made a decision, one of those beyond-recall determinations he would be stuck with for life, an irretrievable moment when a microturn of the wheel and one millisecond would make all the difference, a moment impossible to relive for a different outcome.

He pretended to glance over the back of the seat to look for someone in the rear as he pretended not to notice the woman sitting behind him who was pretending to read.

Then he executed a credible double take. "Oh, hello. Are you going ah—uh—far?"

Devey pretended surprise. "All the way to Charleston. We have to get a ride from there." She went back to her book, pretending disinterest.

"Don't let me bother you—"

"I won't." She smiled without looking up.

Together they decided an uneasy détente was better than pursuit, for the present. She stayed with her book and he went back to his nap, for the present.

As Calley dozed, a light drizzle drifted in from the west, just enough to form puddles and a muddy spray that kicked up from the tires of passing eighteen-wheelers. He was lulled by the rhythmic slap of the wipers as they labored vainly to clear the oily smear in front of Lukey.

Chapter 6

Lenya Leota Klebb was named for a movie star she had never seen. She was 35 when she learned that her namesake was Austrian movie actress Lotte Lenya. She assumed her father, a German soldier, had liked the actress and chose the name because it sounded Germanic. She had no idea that Klebb wasn't her real name either. Her father had chosen it to cover his past transgressions as a member of the Wehrmacht.

Lenya was born after WWII, but she couldn't be certain exactly when. Family records were spotty, and her forged birth certificate said 1950. At times, she suspected she was older, but was able to pass for the age on her birth certificate. But she didn't look her age, whatever it was. Of course, people of her kind could look much younger, or even older than they actually were.

Her mother noticed she was different from birth, but since her father was convinced he was a member of the master race, she didn't mention her condition, and he didn't either. However, by the time Lenya was a year old, it was obvious. Achondroplasia—dwarfism—was the diagnosis, and what followed were denial, rejection, and misery. Her father never accepted her, and often referred to her as "his shame" in front of other relatives.

At puberty, Lenya's physical difference came to be known as "her problem," although it was never a problem for her. Her mother was always supportive, but being married to a brute, her compassion could only extend so far. So, Lenya's teen years were far worse than those of the average adolescent. It wasn't that her father brutalized or abused her, he simply ignored her. If not for her mother, Lenya wouldn't have survived.

When the rebellious teen years arrived, Lenya was as disobedient as any of her peers. She tried to gain her father's attention by shoplifting, drinking, staying out late, and hanging with the wrong crowd. She found her father couldn't care less, and her beloved mother was made miserable by her misbehavior.

Littlefield's Amusements traveled to the nearby town of Hays that fall to play the county fair. For the teenaged Lenya, it was an opportunity to see how the other half lived, and from the beginning she felt a kinship with the folks on the lot. Like her, they were an assortment of people who just didn't fit the mainstream. For hours, she walked the lot, taking in the joints, the talkers, the ride jocks, and the Ten-in-One show. It was all new; it was all amazing.

She stood in front of the Ten-in-One, commonly called a freak show or sideshow, and listened to the talker's bally.

"That's right, folks, a free show right here! Hey you, come on over for the big free show! Gather 'round! Get to where you can see what's going to be happening right here. Right here on this stage, it's all free; it's all starting right now! Everyone's talking about her, you've heard all about her. In just a few moments, she's going to be right up here on this platform, live, before your very eyes."

After several minutes of this, Lenya grew bored and decided to move on. But at that moment, the talker changed pace,
"She's coming out right now! She'll be here in just a minute!"

Of course, she didn't come out at that moment, and as Lenya
once again turned to leave, a tent flap moved in her peripheral
vision.

"Yes-sir, folks, she's alive! She's right here, right now on
this stage. Get up close, move up and get a good look as Littlefield's Amusements proudly presents Antianara the Albino
Pygmy Amazon Queen!"

With that, a bikinied Tamara Kindel ran up the steps and
turned a cartwheel, a back flip, and struck a suggestive pose.
Tammy was the same size as Lenya, maybe slightly taller and
a lot more disproportionate.

I'm prettier than that, thought Lenya.

"I see you got dressed up to come out here," said the talker,
suggesting Antianara wore less when she was inside. She bat-
ted false eyelashes attached to blue eyelids and displayed from
behind large crimsoned lips, a big toothy smile.

"Just one dollar, one-tenth of a ten-spot, a mere pittance—
you can see a whole lot more of her inside. This is a special
price for this very special audience, and will only last for three
minutes. But wait, there's more ..."

Lenya stood and watched as the talker expertly turned the
tip and the crowd began to flow past the ticket stand, leaving
money and hurrying inside, filling the tent with hope.

It happened after the Ten-in-One went dark and she was
walking past on her way off the lot. From the shadows of the
banner and the tent flap, she saw a figure. It spoke. "Are you
with it?"

"With what?" asked a startled Lenya.

"Don't play dumb with me. You ain't no Gilly."

"Wrong. I ain't with no carnival," she replied, "and I ain't playin' dumb neither. You the barker who was out here before?"

"Hon, there ain't no barkers in this kind of show. I'm a talker, one of the best you'll ever hear. Barkers are in circuses. Us talkers are a whole different breed."

Lenya thought, yes sir, a whole different breed apart.

That's how it began. He asked if she wanted to make a lot of money. Talkers put their best lies first. He told her that Antianara's mother was sick, so she was going to leave the show after the fair, going home to care for her. Lenya would never know if this was true.

"If you wanna' give it a shot, I'll work you in while we're still here. You'll get an idea what it's like, whaddya' say?"

"How much does it pay?" asked Lenya.

"We'll talk about that later," the talker cajoled. "You try a couple of shows first, before we talk money. You're over eighteen, right?" He knew she was hooked.

It was a spur-of-the-moment decision, another irretrievable moment, another tiny turn of the wheel or a millisecond that would make all the difference, a moment impossible to relive for a different outcome.

She often regretted not saying goodbye to her mother, but she would drop her a line once in a while when they hit a town that had a post office near the showgrounds. That night Lenya sneaked into the house, threw some things in an old cardboard suitcase, and left, never to return.

Chapter 7

There was no way to tell how much time had passed in the near-darkness of the reading-lamp-lit bus. Calley had curled up in the side-by-side seat, his neck cricked against the window seat's armrest with his feet dangling somewhere out near the aisle. He lay on a soon-to-be numb left arm between him and the seat back, with his right hand gripped through the opening between the window and the seat.

In his dream, he was paralyzed. His left arm was completely useless, and his right hand was reaching far into a rabbit warren where a giant bunny nuzzled his fingertips. It was a warm and sensuous feeling, and he was beginning to dread he had a bestial side that he had yet to explore.

He awoke sort of like the guy who falls asleep in the barracks and awakens to find his underwear filled with shaving cream. It's not a real bad feeling, but it certainly makes you wonder what your body has been up to. As his head cleared, he realized the horned-rim reader in the seat behind him was stroking his fingertips.

Now there was a quandary; should he pull back and be shocked? Should he just remove his hand from the opening between the seat and the wall, or should he try to make some sort of advance? If it was to be an advance, it would have to be done delicately, or he might frighten off the bun—ah—girl.

It took several minutes for him to decide, but there was really no other choice. He advanced his hand slightly. After all, if she quit or complained, it might appear that it was an involuntary movement he performed in his sleep. However, she welcomed the extension and put her hand over his outstretched fingers.

After a few minutes, Calley went for it. He turned his hand and gently took hers. Calley and the woman with no name were now hand-in-hand like star-crossed lovers as they cruised through the starless night aboard the Gray Dog express.

Afraid to move, Calley sat and held the unknown woman's hand for some time before he said anything to her. Finally, after much mental turmoil, he whispered, "Can I come back and sit beside you?"

"Better not," she whispered back. "She's watching."

"I'll go back to the rest room and come back up, and instead of sitting here, I'll sit beside you."

"Okay, just sit like you're talking about the weather. Then you'll have to go back up to your seat."

When he returned, Calley plopped himself into the seat beside The Bunny, who looked up from her book to acknowledge his presence.

"Mind if I sit here?"

"Not at all."

"What about her?" he whispered, nodding toward the dozing woman across the aisle.

"Since some new folks got on and one took your seat, I don't think she'll say anything now."

"I'm Calley, Calley Crowcroft. Glad to meetcha'." He extended his hand.

"Devnet," she said.

"Huh?"

"Devnet, that's my name. Devnet Keavy; it's Irish. Most people call me Devey," she said.

"Oh. My full name is Calais Antonius Crowcroft, but my friends just call me Calley. I don't know what kind of name Crowcroft is," he said almost defensively.

They continued for the next several minutes exchanging information. He learned she was an extremely young-looking twenty-one and decided not to card her for proof. He also learned that Devey was reading *Catcher in the Rye*, and it was her third time through the book.

She quickly learned that Calley wasn't much of a reader, and he'd never heard of J.D. Salinger, and Holden Caulfield was just another name to him.

At some point, Devey gave up on literary discourse, and they spent the next several miles discussing the finer points of whether the Pittsburgh Steelers would be a challenge for the league leaders in a future Super Bowl match up. Devey knew far more about both teams than Calley knew about football in general.

To interrupt the let's-display-our-knowledge turn the conversation had taken, Calley asked about the girl's companion.

"That's my Aunt Sis," she explained. She's a Keavy too, but everyone in the family calls her Aunt Sis. Her name is Siobhan, so you can see why they call her Sis," she said with a giggle. "Those old Irish names aren't as cool as they used to be."

Devey decided not to further the explanation of her aunt's name. She explained that Sis was with her to keep her out of trouble while they had visited a beautician school in Ohio where she wanted to enroll this fall.

"She's kind of like a chaperone?" Calley asked.

"Well, no, more like a nursemaid. That's why I didn't want you to sit here. I'll be up half the night explaining this and giving her a verbatim account of what went on."

"Are you some kind of wild chick who needs supervision when you're away from home?"

"Oh, yeah, yes sir, I most definitely am," she said, squeezing his hand tighter and pulling it close to her.

Chapter 8

Dwarfism. Verne Troyer and Warwick Davis are among the lucky Little People who succeeded in films, but their brethren had a tough time in the entertainment world, particularly since politically correct groups began protecting them. Many lost very lucrative occupations because of this unwelcome "protection." Not every Little Person can be a film star, and none ever find employment in the NBA. Their best opportunities come near Christmas, and Little People must have a hard place in their collective hearts for agents who sell them as elves. But what the hell, it's a living.

"Midgets"—never call a Little Person a midget—are common residents on carnival lots, so common that a midget is seen by other carnies as just another person. But Joey Judd was never seen as "just another person." In fact, he had a personality that prevented fitting in.

He wasn't born in a trunk, but Joey was born into the show. His parents were average height and build, so Joey was a surprise. At first, everyone thought he was cute; a burden the whole family would bear. As he grew older, his parents worked him into their act.

The act opened with his mom and dad prancing onto the stage in tight-fitting body suits. The intent was to make them appear nude. If you were up front, the effect was lost; it was just a man and woman in long underwear. The couple would strike classical poses, many of which required Joe senior to hold Joey's mother off the ground. For its time, it was pretty racy, but audiences soon tired of it, and it became a buildup to a more exciting acrobatic act. And that part included Joey.

At first he rode a tiny bicycle in the act, but the orthopedic problems dwarfism brings soon put a cramp in that part of the family's act. He could ride well enough, but could no longer handle the tricks. He became part of their acrobatic display, but performed less as an acrobat, and was more of a missile.

Joey's persona changed from medicine ball to beach ball to football, and back again. On several occasions, his parents dropped the ball. In one part of the act, each parent grabbed a hand and a foot and swung him back and forth to gain momentum. The target was a net rigged across the stage. More than once, he missed the net and landed hard. More times than he could count, his father simply dropped him on his head. On one such occasion, he was out cold for two days. Perhaps this, along with many disappointments, accounted for part of Joey's temperament.

Joey seemed to age faster than his friends. He was just over three feet tall and had the disproportionate body of what most would call a dwarf. As a youth, he had a full head of blond hair and dark blue eyes, and he considered himself quite the ladies' man. But this didn't last long, and physical problems took their inevitable toll. No doubt the pain contributed to Joey's temperament as well.

He expressed it best to his physician, who suspected Joey's personality was due to depression.

"Look doc, I ain't getting laid. I'm not up for it anymore. I'm crippled up pretty good and don't get around much. I never go on a vacation; it's too much hassle. And folks like me don't tend to live very long. I figure I've eaten more than my ration of shit from this world, so I've decided I'll do what I want and say whatever is on my mind. My ass kissing days are over."

If only he had said, My days of bicycle riding are over.

Chapter 9

Lukey had left the interstate a few miles back, and the smoking bus traveled south in search of oil. The twin diesel tanks weren't about to run dry, but a dashboard light said that it was the oil pan that was empty. The old engine was about to clack its last.

"Don't wanna' get stuck on the four-lane," Lukey announced to no one in particular. "Better we break down on a side road."

The bus veered off a rural exit onto two-lane blacktop, one of the original pre-1980 paved cow paths to Charleston. A couple of college frat rats they had picked up in Clarksburg rubbed condensation off their windows to discover they weren't on the interstate any more.

Under the floorboards, the clacking increased as clouds of black smoke billowed from the rusted exhaust. The oil pressure gauge rose and fell like the mercury in a sphygmomanometer strapped to a gasping geezer's arm. And, like an anxious relative peering at the spastic blips on a heart monitor, Lukey nervously watched the oil pressure gauge and warning light.

In the rear, under the bus, something gave way. A connect-
ing rod, once precision-fitted and oiled to perfection, burned
through its bearings and seized the crankshaft. It broke loose
with a sound that made the previous clacking resemble a ticking Cartier Tankissime. Shortly after, there was an extremely
loud and particularly horrible metallic CLANK as the engine
locked up. Lukey, ever alert to the engine noise, managed to
disengage the clutch and drive onto the shoulder of the road
before they were stuck in the middle of the highway.

One of the passengers rose slightly. "What the Hell?"

"Thrown rod," explained Devey, as knowingly as if she'd
worked the Talladega pits since Charlie Glotzbach burned rubber there. "I expect it went through the block wall, from the
sound of it."

Calley looked at her like a Jack Russell terrier, his head
cocked in amazement.

"Ran into the same thing on the tractor once," she explained.
She described how the old family Fordson blew an engine just
as a stump was being pulled from the tater patch. "Oil went
everywhere. Hit the manifold and started a heck of a fire."

Calley began to wonder what was taking place back there
in the engine compartment. Surely diesel fuel wouldn't be as
explosive as gasoline.

At this point, Lukey, who had gone back to survey the damage, reappeared. "Engine's blown. Gotta' wander down the
road to find a phone. I'll call the office and see if they can send
help."

"How about using someone's cell phone?" suggested one of
the frat rats in the rear.

"You shittin' me? Couldn't hit a cell tower out here if your
ass depended on it. Mainly because they ain't no cell towers.
Hey, if anyone is of a mind to hitch, go ahead. No telling when

they'll get this thing fixed. I know the boss hasn't got another bus. This mess right here is the whole line. You all are welcome to stay and I can tell you for sure that if you go back on the highway to hitchhike, there'll be no refund. It's your call, stay or go."

Calley looked at Devey and Devey looked at Calley. They both looked over to where Aunt Sis was sleeping. It occurred to both of them, at the same time, that no one could have slept through that much noise and confusion. Panicked, Devey fairly crawled over everyone between her and her aunt.

Aunt Sis wasn't asleep. Devey could tell right away because not many people sleep with their eyes open and their eyeballs rolled back up in their head. And, as everyone knows, live bodies tend to stay fairly pink and warm, Aunt Sis was neither. She was gray-green and as cold as a carp. She was most sincerely dead.

Devey slapped her and felt for a pulse at the carotid artery. Nothing. There was no use in trying to revive her; it was far too late for that. By now, Calley had worked his way over to the seat and offered his jacket to cover her. He noticed what appeared to be bruises, but lots of old folks have purplish or brown spots.

"We got a dead woman back here," she announced to Lukey in particular and everyone else in general.

Lukey sighed and said, "Yeah, we get a lot of that on this run."

Devey accepted Calley's jacket and put it over Aunt Sis's head and upper torso. No tears, not a hint of emotion. "Lukey," Devey said, "you need to report the death."

"Yeah, but I got a bigger problem now. I'll call it in when I get a chance."

Devey returned to her seat and Calley sat down and put an

arm across her shoulders. "It's alright," he said, "there wasn't anything you could have done. It's sad but that's the way things happen."

Pretty lame, but it was the best the inexperienced seaman could deliver at the moment. But for Devey, the sympathy was misplaced.

"You didn't know her," Devey said matter-of-factly.

"No, but—"

"She was a real bitch!" Devey scowled coldly. "You didn't know her. This one won't shed any tears. Well, her fare's paid. She can lie there and wait. I sure hope they come before warm weather sets in."

"What are you going to do now?" asked Calley.

"I'm going to sit here a while and see what everyone else does first. I figure them college boys back there are going to get all antsy and hike back up to the interstate. It's just over that hill," she pointed. "We've been running alongside it for miles. Then the others will follow, and pretty soon it'll be me and Lukey sitting here with Aunt Sis for company."

"You gonna' wait for all that to happen?"

"Nope. I'm going back to that outhouse back there, hyperventilate awhile, take a deep breath, then go inside and take a whiz. If you're here when I get back, you can tag along; I think I'm going to take a hike on down the road. We aren't far from the next town."

"Then what?" said Calley.

"I'll see when I get there."

Devey headed for the toilet. She soon returned and gathered her belongings, making sure Missy Anne was up for the trip and stopping for what Calley believed would be a last look at Aunt Sis. Instead, she picked up Sis's handmade purse, opened it and extracted a well-worn wallet. She replaced the purse, stood in the aisle, and shrugged.

"Well she ain't gonna use it," she said to Calley defensively.

Chapter 10

It was another of those irrecoverable, irrevocable, life-altering decisions. Calley wasn't about to pass up an opportunity to trek the road less traveled. He got up just as Devey opened the bus door. He followed her to the steps, then paused, and returned to Aunt Sis. Reclaiming his jacket, he mumbled, "I don't think you'll need this either." He grabbed his AWOL bag from under the seat, strode down the aisle and down the steps, and slammed the bus door on its solitary, cooling passenger. He hurried to catch Devey, already a quarter mile down the road. "Hey, wait up!"

The drizzle reduced to a mist. Fog covered the road in low places. The evening's purple had turned a dense, dark gray. Except for a glow on the horizon, and light dots from a house or two, there was no sign of humanity. The bus, once a refuge, was a fast-fading memory.

They walked side-by-side in silence.

"You'd think a car would'a passed by now," Calley said, just to hear the sound of something besides their footsteps.

Devey set the pace, and Calley hustled to keep up. She said, "If you wait for something to happen, it ain't—never will. If a car comes by and offers, fine, but I ain't gonna' wait. Don't know if I'd want'a ride with anyone stupid enough to stop anyway."

Calley kept up as they quick-stepped the dark highway. Lights approached from the rear, and Devey extended her hitchhiker's thumb.

The car accelerated past as if they weren't there, treating them to a misty spray of slop from the roadway.

"When do you have to be home?" Calley asked.

"No particular time. Don't really care when I get there. Come to think of it, don't care if I ever get there. How about you?"

"I hadn't really thought about it. I don't have to be anywhere at any time. I just got out of the Navy and was going home. I didn't leave anything behind."

"I guess there's no rush then," Devey said.

"My only worries are food and a place to stay. I left my duffle bag on the bus. All I have is underwear and a pair of jeans in this AWOL bag," Calley said.

"I left my suitcase on the bus too. Nothing in it but old T-shirts, blue jeans, underwear, and a nightie," Devey said. "Ain't nuthin' I can't do without. And I sure ain't goin' back for it. I can get by for a few days on what I've got here in my bag."

"What about your Aunt?"

"The bus people can take care of that. I don't want a thing to do with it." She stepped up the pace, emphasizing her deter-mination. "If I stick around, they'll be askin' all sorts of ques-tions, and they'll expect me to take her home. I say, let them deal with her."

"Won't your family give you a load of shit?"

"Never thought of it. Guess I just don't care what they think or do anymore. I don't know if you've ever gotten to that point."

"I have a tag on my duffle bag. I hope it finds its way home somehow. If home is even there anymore."

"Well, you know what Tom Wolfe had to say about that one."

"Tom who?"

"Never mind."

They walked in silence.

Later, she said, "If worse comes to worst, and we have to stay on the road awhile, we can get clothes at one of them do-gooder shops." She smiled at Calley's visible discomfort with the prospect.

"Got any money?" she asked.

"Enough. Why you asking?"

"I've got a good bit that I saved out of the trip and what Aunt Sis had in her purse, but I don't have enough to support your dead ass."

"Don't worry about me. Calais Antonius Crowcroft has been makin' his own way for a long time. Hope you can manage as well as I can."

With that, the couple trudged along in silence as the evening deepened into night, the dead of night.

A glow on the horizon that they expected to be a village or convenience store turned out to be a State Highway barn surrounded by a chain link fence topped by barbed wire. The sulfur glow of the sodium vapor dusk-to-dawners revealed a pasture and the silhouette of a barn beyond. It was well off the road, and the couple, without a word, strode toward it.

Like creatures down the evolutionary scale, they silently bedded themselves in the hay, nesting for the night. With Devey nestled in his arms for warmth, Calley returned her gentle goodnight kiss as he all too quickly fell asleep, dreaming of soft, fuzzy rabbits.

Chapter 11

In the morning, the rabbits scampered away in the twilight, and Calley found himself alone. Actually, he had never felt more alone in his life. He felt panic in the pit of his stomach. Devey had gone on without him.

His watch showed 9:00 a.m. He arose, brushing straw and seeds from his clothing and hair. He ran to the open double doors, hoping for a glimpse of Devey. Beyond the barn, through the morning fog, he saw an ancient, mossy walnut tree and a barbed wire fence that spanned the expanse beyond, but no Devey in the dripping mist.

No matter where he'd been in the past four years, he'd always had someone around. Now abject loneliness overwhelmed him. What now? Back to a main road and find his way south? Back to Dillweed, his homeplace, now changed forever and no longer his home? And who the hell does she think she is with that Tom Wolfe shit?

Calley returned to the barn to lie in the hay, on his back, hands behind his head, and drifted once more into his world that never changed. It was a refuge that didn't know him as a stranger, a sanctuary filled with childhood reminiscences.

"Hey, you lazy shit, are you still in bed?"

Calley didn't know if he was still asleep or not. How had his father gotten in here? Why was his voice so high-pitched?

"I go out and rustle grub for us, while you lay around the house all day. You'd make a fine husband for some desperate housewife someday," Devey said.

"Wha—"

"Look," she announced giggling, holding a bag for him to see. "I found a little diner, Bear Kintry Biscuits, and bought us some breakfast. Hope you like it."

She sat beside Calley. They dined on sausage-egg biscuits and little eight-ounce milk boxes.

"Just like in school," he said as he tilted back the milk carton.

"Milk's not sour enough," she replied, wiping biscuit crumbs from her lips. "You gotta' eat if you're gonna' keep up with me. That wasn't the best roll in the hay I've ever had last night. You poop out too quick."

"I woke up and figured you beat it on down the road without me."

She took his hand and placed it on her knee. "You don't get rid of me that easy. I spent the best part of last night and this morning trying to figure what to do next."

"You really want to hang with me?" he asked. "We make a pretty odd couple."

"Don't get me wrong. Ain't nobody gonna' take care of Devnet Keavy. I make my own way just fine, thank you. I figure if we put what we have together, no, not those things, we can share along. We could say we're married, get jobs, find a place to stay, but not stay in one place too long. We could find ourselves and grow up a little."

"I don't know. I like that part about putting our things together, though."

"Don't get ideas too soon. I thought havin' you along would be something like having a hound dog. Keep me company on the road and keep the other guys off-a my ass. Why not try it awhile? What have we got to lose?"

"Thanks for building my self-esteem. I'll think about it," he said. "Tonight I won't be so sleepy. I'll be all over you like—"

"Not tonight baby doll," she interrupted as she reached into the bag, withdrew a box of tampons, and waved them in his face.

"That's why you're so damned crabby. I thought it was just your personality."

Devey wadded up the empty bag and threw it at him.

"Doesn't the interstate run north-south?" said Calley as he got up and stretched.

"Yeah, but there's a piece between here and Charleston that runs west to east. If we go north, we're into empty country. Why you askin'?"

"I'd like to get off the beaten path awhile," he said.

"Yeah, like old Robert Frost. He took the road less traveled by, and that made all the difference," Devey said.

"Robert who?"

"Frosty the Snowman. Remind me to find us a library. I have recommended reading for you. It's good you dropped out of college when you did. It could have been dangerous—for the college—you might have done some real damage."

"You know, Devey, you don't make real good sense sometimes. Most of the time I don't know what the hell you're talking about."

"I know. Believe me, I know."

Chapter 12

The ambulance arrived, lights flashing and siren screaming. Its vintage was about that of the bus. One would have thought there was an accident victim in dire need of life-sustaining help as the driver and his attendant leaped from the vehicle with life-support equipment in tow.

Instead, the EMTs found a body in need of embalming, quickly. It was early in the day, but flies already dotted the corpse that slumped stiffly in the front of the bus.

The bus driver was busy haggling with a tow truck driver over the cost of getting the bus—now more a liability than an asset—to Charleston. The haggling would go on for another half-hour before the tow truck would hook to the bus and drag it farther south toward West Virginia's capital.

Meanwhile, the EMTs argued how best to get the corpse, now in the first stages of rigor, out of the bus and into the ambulance. The driver, much too fat to be of much help, argued for calling a mortuary and letting them deal with it. The thinner one said they might not see any income if they let that happen and insisted on hauling the body to Charleston. He argued they had to go to avoid missing a payday, so they should take the body along.

After much maneuvering, the pair managed to get the remains of Siobhan Keavy out of the bus with only minor damage to her head, which collided with the door as the skinny guy guided it through and the fat one puffed his way down the steps to the waiting gurney. They expertly steered the wheeled stretcher to the ambulance, loaded her in, and sped away with lights flashing and siren screeching. Freddy "Fats" McKinney, the driver, said he just liked to hear that old siren being given a work out. Sonny "Slim Whitman" McClure pleaded with him to kill it.

Fats shut off the siren well before they reached the Charleston suburbs. Slim paged through a policy manual, trying to find how they were supposed to dispose of the body.

"If it was an accident," complained Slim, "we'd just drop her off at the emergency room, like always. I don't know what to do if they're long dead from something else. Do you know what to do, Freddy?"

"Take her to the county morgue? I'm not sure. Radio in and ask," replied Freddy.

Slim McClure was sure it would be trouble if they had to ask about something they should already know, so they decided to just drive by the morgue and figure it out from there.

"We'll just go in and announce that we've got a body for them. Then we'll just go on, like we know what we're doing," Fats suggested.

Bureaucracies being what they are, they managed to palm off Siobhan "Aunt Sis" Keavy on the obviously addled morgue attendant as they made a hasty departure, siren blaring.

Aunt Sis eventually found her way into a nice, cool stainless steel drawer, where she awaited the medical examiner. She might have had to wait awhile, maybe days, due to paperwork. But Aunt Sis was patient, having all of eternity before her.

Strangely enough, when medical examiner Chauncey Braun heard a new cadaver had arrived, he immediately sensed death by misadventure. He knew nothing was better for his political future than digging into a suspicious death. If only the deceased were a celebrity, or at least a local politician! But that didn't seem to be the case.

Flush with excitement and anticipation, Chauncey scheduled the lab and rounded up an assistant.

"Ignore that bump on the head," said Chauncey. "That's post-mortem, probably by the guys who brought her in. Those purplish marks are from bleeding under the skin," he said to his assistant.

After a quick assessment, the examiner decided to go in. He was interested in stomach and intestine contents, stuff for the lab. After an examination that included the usual stuff—chest, abdomen, brain, he was convinced it was something she ingested.

"I'll get the majors ready for slides and get the stomach contents to the lab while you stitch her up. I'll definitely want to see some liver sections. And I don't think those spots are normal. I'm convinced this isn't your usual old-geezer death."

Chapter 13

No sooner had Calley and Devey reached the stretch of narrow road than a 1948 Chevy pickup coughed and sputtered behind them. They quickly sidestepped to the edge of the asphalt and waited for it to pass. Instead, it wheezed and ground to a halt beside them.

The driver scooted across the bench seat, leaned over and cranked down the cranky passenger window. With some effort and screeching from the winder, the glass screeched four inches lower.

"You folks lookin' for a ride? Where y'all goin'?"

"Where are you going?" asked Calley.

"Ast you first," the driver replied with a chuckle through brown, tobacco-stained lips.

"We really don't know," Calley said honestly.

"Well, you're welcome to get in the back there and ride along with me. But I'll warn ya', I'll hit you up for gas money when we get to a station. I'd let you ride up here with me, but I got my pig with me now. I'd put him in back, but he's prone to jumpin' out."

Devey looked at Calley for a clue as to what to do. She shrugged as a question and as an answer he shrugged in reply. Calley climbed into the rusted truck bed. Devey followed.

Calley leaned around the cab to the driver's window. "I reckon we'll tag along with you and see how far we get."

He rolled the window down the rest of the way. "Watch that window—I never roll 'er up 'til fall. Cain't trust the winder to go up and down all summer." He stuck out a weathered, brown-stained hand. "Name's Gideon Glumphy. Folks just call me Gid."

"Calley Crowcroft and Devnet Keavy back here," Calley replied, grasping a hand that was strong and calloused from years of hard toil.

"A few miles up the road is a general store. Used to have pumps out front. Don't know if it still does. Hope it does. I'm about out," said the driver.

Calley looked at Devey, shrugged, raised his eyebrows, and settled his butt into the truck bed against the cab. Devey shrugged a reply.

The few more miles passed, and no general store appeared. Either Gid's memory had faded or he was confused about which road he was traveling. Sometime around noon, the old truck chugged into the parking area of a less-than-modern con- venience store. It didn't have the appearance of a country store, and it sure didn't seem very convenient. The exterior looked to be bathed in grease, then sprayed with diesel fuel. Signs adver- tised long-gone products, and the gas pumps looked like 1950s antique gas-station memorabilia.

Gid pulled up to the gasoline pumps, and a gentleman who perfectly fit the term "Old Coot" appeared from the store to fill the tank and make sure no gas was stolen. He was an official gas station attendant, because he wore an official gas station attendant's hat of the same vintage as the pumps. The rest of his uniform gave no assurance of his official status: grease-stained bib overalls, unlaced high top shoes, and a flannel shirt.

"Fill'er up?" the coot cackled.

Calley couldn't remember ever having heard this question. To him, all gas stations were self-serve.

Gid shoved the pig all the way over to the passenger's window and climbed out of the cab. "Yep, fill'er up!" Turning to Calley and Devey, he said, "I'm goin' to use the outhouse. You two keep an eye on Winston. He might try to get out my window, and I don't want to wind it up. Might never get it back down."

Calley looked at Devey. "Winston?"

"Gotta' be the pig."

The coot filled the tank and announced to Calley, "That'll be thuty-four, ninety-three."

"You'll have to wait until Mr. Glumphy gets back."

After an eternity of impatient remarks from the coot and one attempted escape by Winston, Gid returned. He said to no one in particular, "That was a rough one. Never eat soup beans and turnip greens together again. And if you gotta' go, do not go in there."

"That'll be thuty-four, ninety-three," repeated the coot.

Gid filched through his pockets and produced an ancient change purse. He unsnapped it and pulled out a wad of bills. He counted out $20 and turned to Calley. "I need fifteen."

Calley gave Devey a hopeful look. She shrugged her now omnipresent shrug, and turned both palms upward. He scowled, pulled out a wallet, and counted it out. After the Coot counted out two pennies and a nickel into the driver's tobacco-stained hand he returned to the driver's side, gave Winston a gentle punch in the snout to move him back to the passenger's side, and got in.

When they were underway, Calley moved closer to Devey's ear. "Just when does this share-and-share alike thing begin?"

"Don't go getting your drawers all in a knot. I'll catch up with you later when we eat or something. Remember who bought breakfast?"

Gid motioned to Calley from inside the cab and Calley leaned around to the open window. "I live just this side of Gibtown and I'll stop when I get to my place. You're welcome to stay with me, or be on your way."

Gibtown, Calley thought, he'd heard of Gibtown from a Navy buddy. That's what they call Gibsonton, Florida, south of Tampa. It's winter quarters and a retirement place for carnival folks. Started when Jennie "the half-girl" and Al "the giant" Tomaini retired from carny life and opened Giant's Camp, a fishing camp near there. Place is full of human oddities. Surely there's no connection between this Gibtown and that one. He leaned around the cab and yelled through the window, "How much farther?"

"I'll let you know before I turn off to my place. It's a few miles past the turnoff to Gibtown, if you don't want to stay with me tonight."

Devey and Calley had already considered being guests of a guy who shared his truck cab with a pig and decided they weren't interested in discovering what sort of housekeeper he might be.

When they arrived at the turnoff, Gid pulled the truck to the side of the road. "Well?"

"I think we're gonna' hike on up the road a-ways and see what we get into," Devey told him.

"Well, you're more than welcome to stay at my place, so if you decide to turn around, I'll probably be up 'til midnight.

Just drop on by. I'll be glad to have y'all as company," he said.

"Thanks, Gid. Maybe we'll stop in town and look for work," Calley said.

"Well, the town ain't exactly on the road. Watch for a red arrow on a sign up that way. Follow that red arrow, and a mile or two after that you'll find Gibtown. Nobody goes up that way much anymore. If they do, they leave real quick. Or, if they don't leave, they seem to stay. I never go up there myself. It has weird vibes. They's folks go up there, and they never come back."

Gid put the truck in gear and elbowed Winston over as he made the turn and headed home.

I meant to ask him how the town got its name, said Calley to himself.

"What?"

"Oh, I was just wondering how Gibtown got its name. You ever hear of Gibtown before?"

"Nope. Not in West by-God Virginia. It's a common name in these parts, though. Maybe Gibson was a politician or Civil War hero."

"Yeah, probably," agreed Calley.

"Maybe it's some kind of *Brigadoon* thing. I suppose you've never heard of *Brigadoon*."

"I'm not that dumb. That's in a musical play. Outsiders can visit it only one day every hundred years. Over in Scotland."

"Yeh, it never changes, and if any visitor stays on and then leaves, the spell is broken, and the whole thing evaporates. I never did like those magical-powers stories. I like stuff that's solid, down to earth, like here and now.

Chapter 14

Soon Calley and Devey came to an intersection with a gravel road with grass sprouting in its middle, clearly it was a road less traveled by. It abruptly turned off to the north, following a deep ravine with banks rising steeply left and right, like the entrance to another land. Sure enough, there was a red arrow, pointing the way up the ravine. The arrow was set at an angle on a speed limit sign. A quarter mile farther was another red arrow, stuck on a bridge abutment. The arrow pointed straight up.

"That must mean straight ahead, because the town sure ain't up in the sky," reasoned Devey. "I hope we aren't just following the directions to someone's party."

"Maybe Gibtown is on another planet, another world," suggested Calley as they walked the gravel road. "Anyway, I don't think we're in Kansas anymore, Dorothy."

Clouds had been forming, then an ominous dark one obscured the sun and the wind was picking up. What was a bright and cheerful day took on a more somber mood.

"Looks like we're in for some weather." Devey looked off to

the west and stepped up the pace.

Ahead, around a blind curve, a shot rang out, startling them. Both knew a shotgun blast when they heard it. As they rounded the curve, a human figure stood at the edge of a cornfield. He was tall, thin, in khaki pants and a denim jacket, wearing a straw hat. Calley thought of the scarecrow in horror movies, and this one stood at the edge of a field of ripening corn against a stormy sky, holding an old double-barreled shotgun.

"How ya'll doin'?" the scarecrow hailed them.

"Not bad. Fixin' to rain. How's yourself?" replied Calley.

"Ready to quit. Not doin' much good out here, and if it rains, I'll just get wet. I'm usually all wet anyway."

The man, holding his shotgun at "present arms" position, was but a few feet from Calley and Devey. He put the gun over one arm and broke it down so that the empty shell casing flew over his shoulder.

"Just not doin' much good at all," he emphasized as the empty whizzed past his ear.

"Bad year for corn? Too dry?" said Devey, hoping to make conversation.

"Good year. Just the right amount of rain."

"So what's the problem?" asked Calley.

"If I was smarter than a crow, I might do some good. Those damned crows. Eatin' it faster'n it can grow. I've tried scarin' them off. Nuthin' works. Can't hit 'em with this thing, but I thought the boom would spook 'em. Nuthin' works. So I'm headin' home before that storm hits. Guess I'm no good as a scarecrow. Just not good for much of anything anymore… dumber than a box of hammers."

The tall man with the shotgun said goodbye and headed quickly down the road they were about to travel.

"He might not be any good at it, but he sure looks the part,"

Calley said. Wonder if he's one of Gid and Winston's relatives."

"He's got the dumb-as-hammers thing down. Maybe so."

The sky had darkened considerably, making it appear to be much later, which added to their anxiety about where they were going to sleep for the night. The landscape opened into a valley with hills to each side, revealing a brighter world on the other side of the ravine, a world that was about to change. On the left were foothills of a mountain range, over which the storm clouds were coming. The breeze cooled and freshened with the first sounds of distant thunder rolling down the valley.

Devey looked up at the dark clouds. "Thinking about turning back?"

"Up to you. But I figure we're just as well off to find a barn or cave. Can you picture us snuggling in with old Gid and Winston for the night?"

"Ugh," said Devey. "We're between a rock and a hard place. Or more like between a pig and a shotgun."

"I think the scarecrow is harmless. Seems friendly enough… bet he's the mayor of Gibtown!"

The breeze escalated to wind and, except for the whine of the wind, a profound quiet settled in. Noisily chirping birds grew silent as their nesting trees swayed, replacing the bird's chirps with a moaning through the branches. In a field below, broomsage rippled as if some giant had thrown a stone in the middle of a large reddish-brown lake. At the end of the field, farther down the road ahead, they could make out what appeared to be a mobile home.

"I'll bet that's a suburb of Gibtown," offered Calley. "I'm guessing the founder is living there, probably Jimmy 'The Crab Boy' Gibson."

"Don't start that carny bullshit," warned Devey. "If they

are carnies, they're sensitive about things. They aren't carnies anyway; they're 'showfolk.' And don't call any of them freaks either. Callie, you're not the most sensitive person I've met."

At this point, Calley decided he'd had enough. He'd played the dumb shit long enough. His eyes rolled, and a temper he didn't know was in him flared and boiled over. Unconscious of the person who was the real, intended target of his invective, he began a spittle-laced tirade. He intended it as an outlet for having to play the fool, but it became a challenge to his father, a defense of his person.

"You think I'm dumber than dog shit, don't you? You wouldn't have let me come along if I'd been a Rhodes Scholar, would you? I might have been a threat to your great ego, your magnificent intellect."

She kept her head down, ducking the wind, pulling her arms across her chest, and kept walking.

Calley ran around in front to block her progress. "Hey, I'm talking to you. I put on that dumb-ass act so you wouldn't think I was just another smart-ass preppie like those frat boys on the bus. Thomas Clayton Wolfe wrote *You Can't Go Home Again*, but *Look Homeward Angel* and *Of Time and the River* are, to my mind, better."

Devey tried to move around him.

"And ... and Robert Frost wrote *The Road Not Taken*. He died about the time all the girls like you were wetting their panties over John Greenleaf Whittier's *Leaves of Grass*."

Tears welled in Devey's eyes, but Calley didn't see them, deep into his rant.

"And Frank Baum wrote *The Wonderful Wizard of Oz* long before Hollywood got hold of it, Dorothy! And I'll bet you've read and know every nuance of James Joyce's *Ulysses*, you literary shit, you."

Devey turned away so he couldn't see the tears.

"'Smatter? Cat got'cher tongue?"

He pulled her around and saw tears now streaming. As suddenly as he had angered, he instantly felt deep regret. He wanted to apologize, but was bewildered in the classic male manner—was she angry with him, or sad that she had taken him for granted? Then he recognized that his audience was many miles away.

Devey stuttered, "It's alright. It's okay, Mr. Super Genius. I guess I deserved it. I really didn't mean—."

Calley interrupted, "No, I didn't mean it. It really wasn't directed at you. There's been too much shit going on in my life...I came on too strong. Got carried away." He put an arm across her shoulder, trying desperately to think of something that would lighten the moment. There was a long, embarrassing silence.

"Can I still be your hound dog?" he pleaded, looking up with Basset Hound eyes.

She smiled through her tears, wiped one eye with the back of a sleeve, and smiled. She petted his nose. "Good boy, Toto." She paused a few seconds. "It'll be alright. But don't think because you read a lot or know a bunch of stuff that you're so smart. There's lots of folks I know who are book smart, but sometimes are dumber than a—a—box of hammers."

"Yeah, and don't go judging folks by they way they look either. I'll bet you thought Gid back there was some kind of hick-boob, the way he talked and the way he was dressed, and riding around with a pig in his lap. Admit it, you did, didn't you?" challenged Calley.

Devey looked shamefaced. "Yeah, I did."

Calley let out a guffaw, and giggling, said, "I did too. I'll bet he can't find his ass with both hands. Dumber than a whole bunch of hammers."

They were at a point where the gravel road was transitioning into a blacktop similar to the one they left earlier. To the north was a driveway that appeared to lead to the mobile home, still some distance away. Oddly, unlike other rural homes, this one had no mailbox at the end of the drive, nor was there a sign to suggest who might live there.

"Do you want to check it out, or go on ahead?" asked Calley.

"Hey, this might be it, Gibtown, for all we know. If we go on we might end up God knows where, spending the night out in the open, in the rain," Devey replied.

And so they started up the steep driveway leading to the trailer beyond.

"If they're little people," cautioned Devey, "make sure you don't call them midgets. They like 'Little People' and consider the other word to be an epithet right up there with the 'N' word. Some of them don't mind 'dwarf,' but you never know."

Putting on his best hick-boob accent, Calley said, "Ah reckon as how they be Munchkins. I'll just call 'em that."

Devey slapped at the air between them. "That's enough!"

Chapter 15

Soon they stood before a doublewide trailer, or as the real estate agents call them, a "manufactured" home. It was neatly painted with meticulous landscaping, flowers in the front near a carport, the lawn neatly mown and edged to perfection. Across the front ran a professionally built deck with redwood and cedar furniture, not cheap resin. Living room lights cast a warm glow onto the deck. Adding to the effect, fog rolled in, accompanied by drizzle, creating a Thomas Kinkade painting, the antithesis of all things carny.

They decided that Devey would knock, and Calley would stand out of the way so as not to appear a threat. She knocked timidly. "Hello, is anyone home?"

Then Devey used her open palm and slammed it against the door. Suddenly it opened to a voice, raspy, loud, like the brass in a heavy metal band. "Geeee-zus! Give me a chance, will ya'? I was all the way in the back, takin' a dump!"

The voice had that heavy-duty Camels-smoker imprint, with a sort-of feminine quality, not smoky-smooth like Lauren Bacall, but a ragged, fine-tuned, Husqvarna quality. And the voice was less than four feet off the floor. Lenya Klebb was short enough to qualify as a "little person."

Calley thought, Hmm, certainly not a Munchkin of my imagination and certainly not a member of the Lullaby League.

"Well, don't just stand there in the drizzle! Get'cher ass off the porch. Get inside and drag that miserable looking mutt or whatever he is with you. If you got any weapons, leave em' out there under the awning."

The interior was startlingly different for a mobile home dweller. Expensive, tasteful furnishings had replaced tacky, trashy trailer furniture. No printed paneling, but drywall everywhere. In the kitchen, particleboard and plastic laminate were replaced with granite-topped maple cabinets, lowered to accommodate the owner. It looked like a professional decorator had spent countless hours planning and purchasing the best.

"Thanks for inviting us in," said Devey.

"This is really, really nice," complimented Calley.

"Yeah, I know," Lenya began. "Gawd knows I spent a fortune getting it to where we could live like regular folks, the Mister and me. It's really a trailer, but we saved real estate taxes, and it's what we were used to."

Devey and Calley looked around for a sign, a picture, some clothing for a clue about "The Mister." Finding nothing, their imaginations began to spin.

"Find yourself a seat. I'll make some coffee to hold us until dinner. You are staying for dinner, aren't you? Sure you are." She imitated W.C. Fields, "It's not a fit night for man nor beast."

Their host wasn't a typical housefrau. Every hair in place, dressed in silk trousers, white blouse, and a light jacket, all perfectly coordinated. She looked ready to step out for an evening on the town when visitors interrupted. Her hair was frosted with touches of gray, courtesy of Mother Nature. Her makeup was nice for her age, which Calley guessed as mid fifties. The only carny cliché so far was the voice and her size.

"This is really great, having company for the evening," she said, over her shoulder to Devey. "If your car broke down and you're on foot, you can use the phone to call."

"Oh, we don't have a car," blurted Devey. "We're on foot. Well, we been hitching along, too."

"Oh," she said in an expressionless voice as she arranged a tray with cups, carafe, and some cookies.

"Please don't think we're a couple of bums," pleaded Devey. "Our bus broke down out on the interstate, and we've been hiking a couple of days now. We have money, and we just decided to travel around a bit and maybe look for work."

"We're no Bonnie and Clyde either," interrupted Calley. "We're just ordinary folks, like uh you."

"Oh, I ain't worried about that sort of thing. I had a couple-a guys in here last year who tried to rip me off. I kicked the shit out of both of 'em and sent them on their way. I sent one off the porch with a 12-gauge load of rock salt in his ass.

"If there's one thing you learn after years on the road, it's how to read people and take care of yourself. Lot'a miles on this old gal, and I intend to put on a few more before I go up to the back lot in the sky. You two married?"

Devey and Calley looked at each other for an awkward moment. "Three long, grueling years," Devey said. "We're about as married as you can get. Oh I'm sorry, we didn't introduce ourselves. My husband here is Calley Crowcroft, and me, I'm Devey Keavy—uh, Crowcroft."

"I'm Lenya, Lenya Klebb, pleased to make your acquaintance. The Mister and me were together for thirty years, some of 'em the best of my life. Others weren't so hot. Ya take the good with the bad, you know."

"Where is he now?" Devey asked.

"He was chopping a tree out back one day and yelled for me. Said he felt paralyzed all over. His heart, ya know. Dropped like a stone and never moved until the undertaker come and got him. Cold as a codfish when they finally came. Oh, I tried CPR. No use, no use. I think that was—let's see—five or six years ago, come this fall.

"That's right. I'm here all alone, so if you start to feel all Bonnie and Clydie, just make your move," she said with a laugh that assured them she was kidding—maybe.

Lenya said her neighbors lived in similar mobile homes and modulars just over the rise behind her place. They all relied on each other for protection and support.

"Ain't nothin' here to steal anyway. I keep my money in the bank, and what I have on hand is a kick just for mad money. You want it, it's yours. There's more where it came from. Most of the furniture is fastened down or too heavy to carry off. I never was much into gadgets. Got a little TV in my bedroom and radio on the nightstand. Gotta' travel light when you're on the road.

"So if you're figuring on ripping me off, go ahead and help yourself, but if you mess with me, you're in for it," she boasted.

They gathered around the table and shared coffee and cookies. Calley was quiet. Devey didn't quite know what to say. But Lenya wasn't the sort to let conversation lag for long.

"You folks don't have a place to stay for the night, do you?"

Devey said, "We really don't, but if you have a spare bedroom, we'd be glad to pay."

"Me and The Mister never took a dime for hospitality in our lives, and I ain't startin' now, so it's settled. I not only have a spare room, I have a guest room with it's own bathroom. How's that? Just like the Holiday Inn!"

"We'll never be able to repay your kindness," said Calley. "Maybe there are some chores I can help with?"

"You never know if you'll be able to repay a kindness or not. If you can't do something for me, then help someone later and pass it forward. Ya see, I believe we're all one family here on this home we call Earth. And if you do something for one of us, all of us eventually benefit. I think it all evens out."

"Karma," mused Calley.

"Hm! Ya don't look like one o' them Hindu fellas," Lenya said.

"He just meant—" Devey began, but thought better of it.

Over coffee, Lenya told them how she and the person she always called "The Mister" had worked the road as showfolk. It wasn't much of a carnival, and the Ten-in-One was more like five standing in for ten. Sometimes she was The Albino Pygmy Princess and did a fire act. At other times, she was Xena the Amazon Warrior, long before that TV skank stole her thunder, and she walked up a ladder of swords and lay on a bed of nails. For a while, she tried running a "mitt camp", palm reading, but got turned off by it. She knew all the mentalist gaff, but thought she really could see what folks were thinking, and got spooked and avoided it.

"We did a little magic act. One that got the crowd going was when The Mister asked someone in the crowd for a watch. He always said he wanted a real expensive one and you know them gillies, that's townies to you guys, would always come up with an expensive one. I'd take it from the mark and, when I handed it to The Mister, I'd pull the old switcheroo. Hand him a piece of junk that he'd put into a bag, smash it with a hammer and make a show of jingling it up and down. You should'a seen the looks on their faces.

"Anyway, he'd hand the bag back to the mark and he'd tell him the trick didn't work. "Sorry," he'd say, "but you can have your watch back." After the guy about shit his pants, he'd tell him to hand the bag to me to see if I could help. I'd do the switcheroo again and the guy would leave all smiles.

"You know what happened in that movie *Nightmare Alley*, don't-cha? The guy was doing a mental act, got carried away with it and became the geek. Didn't want that happenin' to me. Oh, a geek is a down-on-his-luck alky or doper. Bites the heads off a' chickens and snakes, crap like that."

"Ya' know what I'm thinking right now?" asked Calley.

"Yeah," said Lenya. "You think I'm feeding you a big line of shit."

"Amazing!" said Calley. "How did you know that?" He laughed as she returned the laughter in kind, only with more gusto.

She continued by telling them The Mister was one of the world's greatest talkers. "For you folks, that's what you'd call a barker. Circus people might use that word, but none of us ever would. Hell, he'd line up a tip, give 'em the pitch, and turn it so fast he'd empty the lot. The front-end joints would complain he was robbin' 'em blind. Inside, he'd talk 'em into the blow off before they'd catch on to how lame we really were. Before you know it, they were paying a buck to see the pickled punk, and they were out the back and gone. He was so good they started puttin' the Ten-in-One on the left side."

"Sounds like quite a guy," said Devey. She had no idea what a blow-off or pickled punk were, let alone a Ten-in-One.

"He was all that, and more. When times was hard, he'd fill

in on the Ten-in-One and glom some blades, just for shits and giggles. You know that stuff is dangerous. One little slip and one of those swords can give you a nip. First thing you know, peritonitis. No good fix for it back in those days either."

"Anyone hungry? Which of you is the cook?" Lenya didn't wait for a reply, and guided Devey by the shoulder into the kitchen. "I don't know about your man, but mine was only fit for washin' dishes when it came to kitchen work. Looks like he might have other talents, though," she said with a knowing leer.

"How long were you married?" asked Devey.

"Oh," Lenya exclaimed with a laugh, "we never got proper married. We took a turn around the chump twister and that was it. Never expected it to last more than a season, but it just went on and on."

"Chump twister?"

"Oh, I'm sorry. A chump twister is a merry-go-round, you know, the carousel. We called the people on the outside Clems, Gillies, Chumps, all the same by different degrees, anyone who wasn't with the show and in the know. Don't want to call 'em suckers. That's too harsh."

Devey noticed she never got an answer to the question about how long Lenya had been "married." She assumed, correctly perhaps, that Lenya didn't know.

The two women fixed pork chops and gravy over mashed potatoes with green beans. As they worked, Devey kept up with the questions.

"How in the world did you wind up here in Gibtown?"

Lenya explained that she and The Mister just got to be antiques—not really old enough to retire, so they looked for a place that was out-of-the-way. They'd had enough of the road, mud, noise, and most of all, homelessness. So they saved, invested, and looked everywhere for a home.

"What do you mean, antiques? You don't look that old to me," exclaimed Devey.

"Okay, let me 'splain it to ya this way. There's more freaks and geeks out there on the other side of the banner line now than there is inside, under the canvas. Who'd pay to see a fat lady nowadays? Hell, there's more of them than skinny ones. Got 'em riding around in little carts at the shopping malls, too fat to walk. And, would you pay to see some guy covered with tattoos when you can just go to any biker meet? We had a guy who would pierce his tongue and drive an icepick through his arm. Pretty tame shit these days.

"We could see the road life drying up. Carnivals were becoming more like museums, and we saw ourselves as antiques on display. Between the late '60s and the '90s, it just evaporated. In 1997, Royal American, now there was a class act, staged its last show. That was the end, as far as I was concerned. Some shows are still out there, but it's not the same." She turned away and dabbed at an eye with her apron.

Lenya explained they decided on this part of West Virginia because hurricanes, tourists, and retirees were beating up Florida, the other Gibtown. In West by-God Virginia, the weather wasn't really cold in the winter or very hot or humid in the summer. Most of it was off the beaten path, and the folks were independent, known for being outspoken. They liked the State Motto, *Montani semper liberi*, "Mountaineers are always free."

"West by-God ain't crowded, and don't have much grief from hurricanes or tornadoes. And we don't even live in Gibtown proper. That's a place in Florida, Gibsonton. A lot of showfolks, a lot of Royal American refugees retired there, and it got the moniker, Gibtown, and it got known for the human oddities, freaks, who hung out there.

"I found out the name from some other showfolk, and thought it would be funny to live in Gibtown, West Virginia. On down that road you just came off of is Gibsonton, named after the family of a state senator's wife. Since there's some showfolk who live outside of town and a few in town, so people started calling the whole shebang Gibtown. Anyway, the town proper is on down the road. If Gibsonton was a town, you'd be in its suburb, but it ain't big enough to have one, and this part ain't really called nuthin'."

Devey busied herself with the potatoes, and Calley helped Lenya set the table as she continued what had developed into a monologue.

"Only about 500 people all together. Ain't even on the map, and there's some pretty small nowhere-no-hows on the map! They're pretty self-contained and self-sufficient over there. Don't warm up to strangers very quick, and I don't go any more often than I absolutely have to. You kind of get the feeling they're up to something, like a cult, or like that. It's weird, like they don't want you around.

"Don't get me wrong, I don't think they're a bunch of devil worshippers or dope growers or anything such as that. Uh, I mean like commercial growers. Just about everyone grows their own nowadays. I quit smoking after The Mister passed. Think it was what did him in. Never got into the dope. Y'all don't smoke, do you?"

"We never started," Calley said.

"Good," she exclaimed as they seated themselves for dinner. "Now does anyone want a prayer? I'm here by myself mostly and usually say grace by myself."

Devey looked at Calley. Calley was the one that shrugged this time and said, "Why not? Go ahead."

Lenya bowed her head and waited until the spirit was upon

her. "God's neat. Let's eat!" she proclaimed, and dug into the mashed potatoes. Immediately, lightning struck nearby, thunder rolled across the valley, and rain began pummeling the roof. Devey ducked, wondering if God was offended.

Chapter 16

Even 10:00 in the morning seemed to come quickly for everyone in Lenya's home. After breakfast, she offered to introduce them to her closest friend and neighbor.

"I'll tell ya upfront, don't make fun of the man! He's had a hard time in life and he don't need it any harder. He has a nervous condition, and he's earned every bit of it. I think he's a, a uh, paranoid, schitzo-wacha-ma-call-it. At least that's what his friends say. I think they call it bi-polar or some such now.

"A few years back he was workin' his swaypole act in front of a crowd at a county fair."

"I know I have a lot to learn, but what's a swaypole?" asked Calley.

"I think they're made of aluminum and all that I've seen are 65 feet high. There's an outfit in Germany that has one over 204 feet, but these days everything has to be bigger and higher."

She explained that swaypoles are rigged to stand vertically and performers climb to the top to perform. On the way up, they may do handstands, put both hands on the pole and stick their body out to the side. Once at the top, they usually have a cradle or some fixture where they do handstands, headstands, and work with a partner. During the whole routine, the pole sways back and forth.

"Sometimes they use two swaypoles together, flying from one to the other. Leon—that's the guy you're going to meet— Leon Riluttante and his partner Lynette would climb the pole, and that's no mean feat. They were known as Lynette and Leon, 'King and Queen of the Air.' The boss just called 'em the Daredevil Dagos. Folks weren't as sensitive about names back then.

"Just climbing that sucker would wear me out, but about the only danger is making a mistake, and you'd probably make only one. The performers are usually looped or tied to it some-how. It's one of the safest aerial acts there is. Anyway, they were out there with a crowd of about 10,000 and were about finished with their act when the pole snapped. That's the big-gest danger, and it's one of those things you just can't predict. When it snapped, Leon went flying right into the canvas of a joint nearby. But Lynette fell straight down and was impaled on the remaining part of the pole. Killed instantly. Not a pretty sight for the kiddies."

"Oh, that's terrible!" said Devey.

"Not for Leon. He was knocked out for two days. I imag-ine some folks are still having nightmares over it, though. It was quite a mess. I always think about the kids who see those things.

"So, after a long recovery, Leon finally left the hospital and had to deal with Lynette's death. He was grief-stricken for months, and didn't so much as try to climb a swaypole again for nearly a year. Finally, he got up whatever it takes to give it a try. At first he just walked around checking the cables, the rigging, that holds it up. He'd pound the pole with a hammer, testing it, and he'd tap the cables with a wrench. Then he'd just walk away for days at a time.

"One day Leon came out and walked to the base of the pole, chalked up his hands and started to climb. He made maybe six feet before he slid back to the ground. He hung his head, walked away, and never returned. He took what was left of the pole Lynette was killed on and made a sort of macabre memorial out of it."

"Got every right to be a little screwy, I think. He's earned it," offered Calley.

"After that day, I never saw him again until I moved here. He lives in a small place over the hill. Please, don't mention any of this when you see him, and please don't ask him what he did in the show. The poor man has been through so much … he's gone funny in the head, and keeps talking about how the Mafia are trying to find him, and that he knows the FBI and CIA are in on it, whatever it is.

We won't stay long. I just want to show up to introduce you. Don't want him to feel left out, you know?"

The three visitors knocked on Leon's door and met the shell of a man Lenya had told them about. Everyone was so uncomfortable that they stayed only briefly. Calley and Devey got the feeling it was a pro-forma visit anyway. The visit was something Lenya felt obligated to do, and Leon seemed relieved when they said they had to go.

"I'd go over and see Sam Bowler, but he's been down at his cornfield for the last couple of days. Says he's having crow trouble this year. Instead, let's go over there," Lenya said, directing their attention to a doublewide about fifty feet away.

Chapter 17

Chauncey Braun studied the lab workup on Aunt Sis for several minutes. He reached for a calculator and punched some numbers, hit CLEAR, and entered some more.

"Hey, Maude, get in here. I want to bounce something off of you."

Maude Helphenstein, near-retirement, receptionist, investigator, lab rat, and all-about flunky, arose from her chair to answer her master's call.

"You seen this lab report?" asked Chauncey.

"You know I ain't supposed to look at those things before you do."

"Don't try to bullshit me. I know you saw it. I just want your opinion. I have an idea of what killed her. I just want another viewpoint to see if we came up with the same idea."

"All right. I think Siobhan Keavy was poisoned. There was arsenic in her. That's proof enough for me she was murdered."

Chauncey frowned. "Don't think so. There's a lot of arsenic in well water and the general environment, the power plants and such. If she was around it at work or somewhere, she

83

could have gotten into it, or rather, it into her."

He tapped the report with his pudgy forefinger. "Did you notice the amount of digitoxin there? She might have used it on her own. Some old folks use it for heart—"

Maude interrupted. "How the heck would she get that stuff?"

"Simple. It comes from a common wildflower, foxglove. Available to anyone who knows what to look for. I'll bet she used herbs and natural medicinals. Some folks use foxglove for chest pain."

"So, do you think she was murdered?" said Maude.

"I don't think it was that at all."

"You think she was dosing herself with foxglove?"

"Not enough of it to be fatal. No, I think I know what did it. You know what used to be in rat poison?" Chauncy asked.

"Yeah, warfarin. But they use it as a blood thinner now, Coumadin, ain't it? Didn't they take that out of rat poison?"

"Yep, but the old gal's got enough of the new stuff in her to do her in. The newer stuff is brodifacoum. I'll bet someone was giving it to her in capsule form. Put it in her vitamins, I'll bet. Accounts for the hematomas, no doubt."

"So now what?" Maude asked.

"Guess I'll call the State Police. I'll have to file the papers to start an investigation. We'll have to contact her next of kin. See what they can tell us."

Within a few hours, the authorities learned about the Keavys of Madison, West Virginia and that Devnet Keavy had been traveling with her Aunt Siobhan Keavy on a trip to Ohio. They also learned that Devnet Keavy had been missing for two days. Devnet had abandoned her aunt, and then disappeared. Talk about red flags for the investigators.

"Madison Woman Wanted for Questioning" headlined the

Charleston Daily Mail. Although the county had jurisdiction, authorities there gladly handed off the case to the State Police. Everyone knew the FBI could be involved sooner or later if kidnapping was suspected.

Chapter 18

Lenya and her new-found friends spent the day cruising the town, sometimes just stopping to say hello, sometimes staying a while, but never getting really acquainted with anyone in particular.

"One more visit, friends," said Lenya. "I saved this one for last. Joey Judd is the epitome of the nasty little prick midget. He's something else and for the most part, I can only take him in small doses."

Joey wasn't particularly vicious, but he simply took no shit from anyone. He could never accept that he usually was the smallest man in the room. When Joey moved to the back lot of Gibtown, one of the first residents he met was Leon Riluttante. Initially there was a brief lapse in Joey's vitriol, and they got along okay. But soon the two men found they shared both a mutual hatred as well as a lasting friendship. Like an old married couple, they would have knockdown, drag-out verbal tiffs. But when a tiff was over, one of them usually said, "So, you coming over for chess on Tuesday?"

Lenya knocked and waited. "He's probably back in there jerkin' off,' she said with a snicker. "Little jerk-off."

"Who's out here bangin' on my door?" called Joey. "Oh it's you, shorty," he said to a woman who was inches shorter than he was as he appeared in the doorway. "Who ya got there with you?"

"A couple of new folks. They're gonna stay with me awhile. I was sort of walkin' 'em around, introducing them to my friends. After we met all my real friends, I thought they should meet the town's biggest asshole, so here we are."

Joey looked up at Devey and Calley and extended a hand that sprouted stubby fingers.

"I'm Joey Judd—the asshole. Don't mind Lenya. She's had a hard-on for me ever since I turned her down one time."

"Joey Judd, you lying son-of-bitch," Lenya said with a grin. "If you weren't smaller than me, I'd drop-kick your midgety ass into the next county."

"Yeah, and if you weren't a woman—" He turned to Devey and Calley, and stage-whispered aside, "I think she's a woman, can't tell by lookin', though!"

"When you coming down to dinner? It's been a long time," offered Lenya.

"I just got over the shits from the last time. I'll be down in a week or so."

As they walked back to Lenya's house, she abruptly said, "I got more room than one person needs. You want to stay with me? You set a fair rent, and you won't have to pay one thin dime until you find jobs. I could use a little extra money. How's that sound?"

Calley protested, "That's too kind of you Lenya! We don't want to take advantage." Devey drilled him a lethal look.

Lenya shrugged. "It gets lonesome out here. I could use the company. You'd do me a real favor if you'd just—just take advantage of me!"

"You got a deal," Devey quickly interjected. "We'll stay at least until we can earn enough for a place of our own or we decide to move on."

Lenya's home had resumed its Kinkade-esqe hominess in the fading light. A porch light guided them home, and a lamp gleamed through a living room window. The air had cleared, the rain clouds moved on, and the sky reflected the afterglow of day. Birds twittered their last twitters as they roosted, and crickets joined the evening anthem as quiet settled in around the little place that was now a home for three.

"G'nite, momma," said Calley.

"Good night, John Boy," answered Devey with an unseen smile.

Chapter 19

Near Orlando, Florida there is a town that grew from Disney-think, a planned community that caters to nostalgia, sentiment, and luxury. There you can still buy a new antique Victorian look-alike house for less than half a million in a complete, pristine, cookie-cutter community, all architect designed, chosen from the pattern book. It's a setting in which you expect to see Stepford wives at any turn, Celebration, U.S.A.

A little farther north, between Orlando and Ocala, is The Villages. It features gates, golf carts, fairways, and lots and lots of white people playing at being retired. In The Villages, the Stepford wives give way to the Red Hats. As old as the residents are, it was reported that The Villages had a serious problem with sexually transmitted diseases. "Viagra," the news announcer explained.

Life in Gibtown, the West Virginia Gibtown, not the Florida one, is somewhere between these two. It has all the vinyl-stucco, faux marble, printed wood of both Celebration and The Villages, but none of their panache. And no one in Gibtown would call it that. They much prefer Gibsonton. They even consider "Gibtown" an affront. It isn't that they're uppity or snooty;

they just never seem to consider others, except as furnishings for their own existence. Gibsonton, West Virginia residents make the "me generation" seem solicitous by comparison.

The West Virginia Gibtown sprang almost fully formed, overnight. Being in a remote part of a remoter state, many legal and social niceties were ignored. Subdivision plans, environmental impact studies, historical, archeological, and geological preservation didn't bother developers, who knew that it's much easier to ask forgiveness than permission, especially when the land you're developing is too far from the beaten path to be visible. A squeaky bureaucrat is easily greased with a bit of cash. In these parts, a thousand dollars has the impact of millions elsewhere.

The main obstacle to development in the state, if he chose to be an obstacle, was Senator Christopher Wren. Campaign contributions, plus naming the main street Wren Way, plus naming the cross street Christopher Boulevard assured a blind eye toward the Gibsonton Project. The deal was sealed when the town adopted the maiden name of Senator Wren's wife— Gibson. No one would ever say "Gibtown" in the Senator's presence.

Wren not only accepted this new village in his state, he gave it his imprimatur and pulled some pork for the town's infrastructure. He made sure that Gibsonton got federal funding for a sewage treatment plant, and that the plant sported 2-foot-high illuminated letters
ARCH MOOCH MEMORIAL FACILITY
in recognition of his dearest political enemy.

Maybe that's why some believed the development to be some government-funded commune, a quite reasonable suspicion in West Virginia. In 1933, as President Roosevelt worked to heal the Great Depression, he created a planned community named Arthurdale. It was a village for displaced and broke coal miners, and it became a pet project of the President's wife, Eleanor. It was a social experiment in communal living that today some might call an experiment in socialism, or even communism. Today, much of Arthurdale is a ruin and as in just about every experiment of this sort, capitalism returned with a vengeance.

Gibtown was a gated community far removed from that model. A landscaped brick wall, hidden by ivy and tall cedars, was built for nearly two miles across the front of the town. It extended on both sides to points beyond sight. There the handsome brick turned to chain link, with brambles at the bottom and disguised razor wire at the top. The wire, held in the mouths of friendly teddy bears, sat atop each post. Video surveillance cameras and electronic sensors, hidden in the bears, guarded the perimeter.

The gate was a friendly portal with a WalMart style greeter who waved, smiled, doffed his hat to the ladies, and wished all a good day. The gate wasn't to keep people out or in. It was a funnel in the perimeter that gathered information on who arrived and departed. The friendly gatekeeper had a photographic memory that retained license numbers and car descriptions until he quickly ducked into the booth to dump his information into his computer, in case the video failed or the information required immediate access.

The official reason for the fence is that it deters an unmanageable deer herd, protects the lawns and landscape, and secures residents from non-existent crime.

Gibtown's developer/manager was Mountainaire Enterprises, LLC, which went by "ME," causing some confusion: if anyone asked who was in charge, the answer was always "ME." Search the Internet for the company, and you are out of luck. Search for Gibsonton, WV and you also come up dry. No map reveals its existence, either. It's like Russia's closed city of Sarov, a nuclear R&D site they didn't remember to mark on maps.

There's only one intimidating indication, if you're sensitive to such things. Near the gate, almost obscured by a large barberry bush, is a sign:

MEMBERS OF THE MEDIA
Please register with the attendant

But visitors are rare and no one can recall ever registering a member of the media. Behind the gate, Gibsonton was neat, clean, manicured, and landscaped to perfection. Unlike many similar gated communities, where a variety of architecture is encouraged, all of the houses were Victorian era, some plain, some elaborate. They were arranged around a town-market square, with a large clubhouse at the far end, and the gatehouse on the other. Satellite antennas are considered an ugly nuisance and aren't allowed.

Like satellite antennas, small children and large dogs aren't in Gibsonton either, perhaps for the same reasons. An absence of kids in a retirement community is not odd.

Gibtown's missing satellite antennas, missing children and large dogs, created a cloistered existence, and a population living an idyllic life, removed from the madding crowd—apart, almost sheltered—adding to the ambiance that locals who know about the place call "weird vibes."

Or as Gid so aptly puts it, "There's something about Gibsonton that's out of kilter."

Chapter 20

Calley awakened to the noise of a busy kitchen. He felt the empty depression in the mattress, and it was cool, Devey had vacated it a while before. She and Lenya were busily preparing breakfast.

As he entered the dining area off the kitchen, Lenya warned, "Siddown and stay out of the way, and keep yer damn fingers outta' the bacon!"

"Where do you get groceries around here?" Calley asked. "We should at least be paying for the food."

"All in good time, all in good time. I'll let the both of you go to town and get some stuff a little later. You'll hav'ta introduce yourselves, 'cause I don't know nobody over there anyway. It's all we've got for a store for miles."

They ate, and the women sat back and gave Calley an expectant eye. He returned with upraised eyebrows and a questioning eye.

"Don't play dumb," said Lenya. "We fixed it; you mop it."

"Sure," Calley said obediently as he grabbed a too-small apron and went to work. The women cleared the table and scraped dishes.

"You get a newspaper?" asked Calley.

"Nope. Pick up a Sunday paper at the store if you want to catch up."

Calley and Devey saw that outside news was of little interest in this isolated community. Lenya said "the country" when she actually meant the world, the nation, or the government. Most folks just referred to things elsewhere as "out there." Carny folks in the suburbs called Gibsonton "over there," or "uptown." Once they'd been in Gibtown awhile, they lost interest in what was "out there." The universe of Gibtown folks was Gibtown. Their TV was provided free by Mountainaire. It consisted of all local news, chat, TV-Land entertainment, and old movies.

Calley and Devey started to walk the mile into town for groceries. Once out of Lenya's hearing, Devey asked, "What do you make of all of this?"

"I dunno. I like Lenya a lot—brassy and mouthy, but I like that in an older woman."

"Oh, yeah?"

"You know what I mean. What you see is what you git. You don't like it, tough shit."

"What about Leon?" Before Calley could answer, she continued. "Did you ever have a class in Italian?"

"No, why?"

"Just wondered. Did you know that Riluttante means 'reluctant' in English? It dawned on me that you could translate Leon Riluttante into 'Cowardly Lion.'"

"You're really into the *Wizard of Oz*," Calley joked. "And there was the Scarecrow we saw popping of his shotgun not too effectively."

"Hmm. I wonder if Lenya's husband—he froze up while chopping wood—had anything to do with tin."

"When we get back, I'll ask her."

"No, I'm only teasing! If you do, I'll tell her you're wondering if the Mister's normal-size shlong seemed overly large to her."

Calley grinned at her. "I think you have a shlong complex, but I'll keep my mouth shut. And besides, what makes you think it was normal size?"

They continued to walk and discuss Oz parallels. They mutually decided that they were still in West by-God, and there was no denying it. Oz was another place all together, maybe in Gibtown.

Chapter 21

As they approached the Gibtown gate, the gatekeeper stepped from his booth. "Hiya' folks. Stoppin' by for a visit?"

"Going to the store for some things," replied Calley. "Maybe walk around the square and see the sights."

"You're more than welcome. The store's about three blocks up that way." He pointed through the gate. "Ya might wanta' take a look around first, so you don't have to drag your groceries through town. Leave your cart here, if you like. I'll keep an eye on it for you."

Devey whispered, "Seems friendly enough."

"Take your time, but do me a favor and head back out here before it gets dark. The little old ladies will be calling me about strangers prowling around, if you know what I mean."

"We'll just be a couple of hours," Calley said.

"Take your time, no rush."

Calley and Devey strolled around the square until they found the ME Grocery and glanced through the front windows. "Not a broad selection, but more than expected. The prices are right," Devey said.

Soon they found themselves in the front of a row of small

lots with fairly large homes. Calley looked for names on mail-boxes. Few people "out there" put their names out in public, but Gibtowners found no reluctance in doing so. One yard had a large stone emblazoned with the name NICOLETTI. Across the street a yard sign read THE ROSELLI FAMILY.

"Little Italy?" whispered Devey.

"Or Gibtown's Mafia Corner. Don't make too much of the Mafia thing. They imported a lot of Italians into West Virginia to work in the coalmines back in the 1930s. Italian names are common as dirt in some places."

"That must not be Mr. Roselli coming out of the house, unless you know some redheaded Welsh Sicilians," observed Devey.

"Probably someone visiting."

Most Gibsontonians appeared to have stepped from a '50s or '60s movie. And they didn't look wealthy enough to afford Gibsonton. People seemed to be in a hurry to be in a hurry; no passing the time of day. They didn't seem more than a rung or two socially above Lenya and her neighbors. And they weren't nearly as friendly as the carnies "out there."

They finally looped back to the store for their groceries. "I'll run down to the guard shack and get the cart. I'll be right back," Calley said.

In the store, they tried to chat with the checkout clerk. He was having none of it.

"You live around here?" Devey asked.

"Nope. Live up the road a piece." "A piece" can be from a few blocks to ten or fifteen miles. Perceiving that any attempt to pry anything but basic yes and no answers out of the clerk, Devey didn't pursue the conversation. However as they were handed their change, the clerk did take a moment to caution the couple. Perhaps it was his intention to be friendly, but he was more perplexing than helpful. And he added, "Folks who live here mind their own business, and they don't take kindly to strangers askin' about them. Everyone's here because it's where we want to be. We didn't just happen here, ya know."

Perplexed, they left the store. "I feel like we're aliens!" exclaimed Devey.

Discretion, more than anything, hastened an end to the couple's visit to Gibtown. It seemed almost as if they had—as aliens from another planet, landed in a flying saucer and found themselves in the middle of those "They-walk-among-us" 1950s movies like *Invaders From Mars*.

They found their way out of "over there" long before the sun set. Calley admitted he had visions of blue-haired little old ladies getting up from a Canasta party to drive them from their midst with frying pans and pitchforks in their hands. "Definitely not the Emerald City or Oz," Calley said. "Makes me wonder what the hell they got going "over there.""

Chapter 22

His name was really Barnard Pipare, but he used the name Barry. If you wanted to start something with him, call him Barney and you would see his vicious side. Barry Pipare had one of those names that was too memorable for his own good — useful if he ran for office, but he didn't. He was a state investigator on his way up. Being at the bottom rung, it was the only direction he could move.

He had driven a black, unmarked Crown Vic all the way up from Charleston, with orders to pick up some woman and deliver her to the courthouse at Grantsville. A damned taxi driver for crackers, wood hicks, he thought. Well, you gotta' start somewhere.

Shadows were lengthening when he turned off the interstate onto the road that seemed to be the back way to nowhere. He'd heard of the carny people who lived in this God-forsaken area, and he was about to experience them first-hand. His mission was to take into custody one Devnet Iris Keavy. Following directions to the carny camp, Barry found Lenya's driveway and stopped by the deck.

Hearing his car, Lenya and Devey walked around to the

driveway. "You expecting anyone?" Lenya asked. "Looks like a police car. Not marked' though. Bet he's lost."

"I hope so, but I'll bet he's looking for me," Devey replied.

"Either of you Devnet Iris Keavy?" he asked.

"I'm Devnet."

"You have an aunt named...So-by-han...no, Shoe-ban... er...Chopin...or somethin' Keavy?"

"Yes."

"Well, your aunt's deceased. We need to ask you some questions. So I'm here to take you over to the county seat."

"Am I under arrest or something?"

"No, they just have some questions. However, if you don't come by your own volition, I'm authorized to place you under arrest."

"Guess she's got no choice then, does she?" Calley had just stepped out the door. He squinted at the investigator. "Hey, ain't you Barry Pipare from down near Dilweed? How in the hell are you?" he said, holding out his hand.

"Well, I'll be damned! If it ain't old Calley Crowcroft. I ain't seen you since you took off to join up with Uncle Sam. Ain't you a sight for sore eyes. It's good to see you. Although I don't care much for the circumstances of the visit," Pipare said as the two men shook hands and hugged.

"Ah...we'll have time for a reunion later, if we can find a bar," Calley said, laughing. "This here is my wife, Devey," he said, pointing. "And that one there is Lenya Klebb. Two of the finest ladies you'll ever meet."

Calley pulled Barry away from Devey and Lenya and whispered, "Ain't really married." Then, "What's all this about?"

"Her aunt died on that bus that broke down. And Calley you know as well as I do, you can't just up and walk away from something like that! The state's got questions that need answering. Seeing as how you're not married, I can't take you along with her. Shit, Calley! I'd like to, but my ass would be in a sling if anything happened. Hope you understand."

Calley nodded, and Pipare turned to Devey.

"Okay, Miss Keavy. You want to take anything along, get it together now. You'll be away a couple of days. After that, who knows? I have to keep an eye on you while you gather your things. If you want to use the bathroom, close the door, but I'll be right outside."

Devey packed Calley's AWOL bag with a few things, including Missy Anne, put on some lipstick, and got ready to leave. Calley asked, "Can we have a few minutes?"

"Sure, just don't take too long. I want to get back."

The couple slipped into the bedroom and closed the door. "Listen," Calley said. "Soon as we go back out there with him, while we're all together, tell him you want an attorney. They have to give you one, and I think it's free. They can't hold you and make you say anything unless your lawyer is present. I learned that much from TV. This won't amount to much, and it'll be over with in a day or two and we'll all be back together."

"Easy for you to say."

"Listen, I've had my scrapes with the law. Just watch what you say, and it'll turn out all right."

"Yeah, you had your teenage scrapes with the county laws, but you never killed anybody, now did you?" Devey blurted tearfully as she bolted for the door.

Calley felt a horrible sinking feeling, memory flashing to his bloated brother's corpse and to Aunt Sis with her eyes staring blankly. He assumed Devey was feeling guilty for leaving her aunt the way she did. Surely there was no way she could be blamed for some old lady dying on the bus.

They walked to the car. Barry opened the back door on the passenger's side. Devey entered, and Barry made sure her seatbelt was secure. Then he climbed behind the wheel. If Pipare were white, Calley wondered if he would have let Devey ride up front with him. Maybe it was one African-American's way of avoiding trouble in the land of the too white. They slowly drove down the driveway—driving miss Devey.

Chapter 23

Calley and Lenya stood as the car disappeared. Lenya broke the silence. "All right, time for a stiff drink. That's what I do instead of crying. Haven't had a good drink since The Mister passed. Think I still have some of his Courvoisier."

Lenya found glasses and filled them halfway with the golden cognac. They sat at the dining table until late afternoon turned to evening, and laughter turned to tears and back to laughter again, as both sampled too much and traded the small talk of the nearly drunk.

"So you and the cop were tight back in Virginia?" Lenya asked.

"You askin' because he's a cop, or because he's black?"

"Don't get your biggoty bowels in an uproar. I thought you Southern boys didn't get along with them folks. And you don't strike me as one who'd get along with the law either."

"I don't like being stereotyped. In any event, we got along just fine—until today. I'm getting awfully sleepy," he said with a yawn. "I'm off to bed."

"Sort of a double for a young Denzel Washington. I think he's cute," she said as Calley hurried down the hallway.

As Calley drifted off, he started at a quiet rap on the bedroom door. "Can I come in a minute?"

Calley scowled. "Sure."

"I just can't sleep," she said. "Maybe if we could talk a while."

Lenya perched on the edge of the bed. She reminisced of the days when the carnival was new, when the lights were bright, the paint on the rides was unmarred, and the seats weren't dirty and torn. The banners were freshly painted and the canvas had that newly waterproofed smell. Even the kootch show seemed more like Broadway to her then, than the midway it really was. Even the sawdust had the smell of new pine.

She spun a whole, sad story about the days when the show began to fade, and some of the bulbs across the banner burned out and were never replaced. She told of the day the mentalist finally melted down from dope and became the show's full-time geek.

"I'm kind'a woozy. Do you mind if I lie down here a minute?" And Lenya lay beside him.

Soon Calley put his arm around her. When she didn't protest, he pulled her closer, and she snuggled against his warm body. Eventually he cupped her breast in his hand as she murmured and moved even more tightly against him. Their being together was sensual, but at the same time platonic, suspended somewhere between arousal and the simple enjoyment of the closeness of another human spirit. Quietly as if kissing a child good night, Calley brushed her hair aside and gently kissed her cheek. They lay there, and Lenya dozed while Calley fell into a deep, dreamless sleep.

When Calley awakened, Lenya was gone. Her warmth remained, telling him she had only recently left. And they made an unspoken pact, each to themselves, never to speak of their night together.

The morning was bright and full of promise. Birds sang and robins chased worms on the lawn. None of last night's somber tone remained, although a kind of melancholy hung over the morning coffee.

"Wonder if they'll keep her long?" pondered Lenya.

Chapter 24

The next evening, the Crown Vic pulled into Lenya's drive-way. Barry Pipare sat properly in front, and Miss Devey sat primly in the back.

Bag in hand, Devey got out and ran to Calley's outstretched arms. "I'll tell you all about it later," she whispered in his ear.

Pipare explained, "They held her overnight, but it didn't amount to much. The officer took a statement and asked a few questions. That's all there was to it. If she hadn't asked for a Public Defender, we would have been back here the same evening. Pretty cut and dried." Devey was nodding in agreement and smiling.

"Calley, I'd like to stick around and have that reunion, but I gotta get the car back. Got a phone number? I'll give you a call."

Pipare offered a couple of his cards. "Keep one and write your number on the other. Put your e-mail on there too."

Lenya laughed. "You gotta' be shittin' me." She wrote her number on the card and returned it.

"Duty calls," Barry said and went to the car. "You call me now. If you don't, I'll call you." With that, he started rolling down the driveway.

"I expect we'll see a lot more of him," Devey said so Lenya couldn't hear.

They listened to Devey's cursory account over dinner. "They assigned me an attorney. They asked about my relationship with Aunt Sis and the circumstances of her death. There's really not much to tell. I didn't like my aunt much, and she died on the way home from a trip to Ohio. That's about it. But I'm tired and heading for bed."

Devey also related that the state didn't put her in jail overnight, but they had provided her with a nice room in a motel nearby. The motel had a decent restaurant, and the state provided her with meal tickets for her dinner and breakfast. She ate lunch with Barry Pipare before they headed back to Gibtown.

At the end of the meal everyone agreed they needed rest and Lenya said she was going to read until she got sleepy. Calley and Devey headed for the guest room, Calley filled with anticipation about hearing the details of the "inquisition."

They closed the bedroom door. Calley said, "Okay, spill it. What really happened?"

"Well, they didn't actually say it, but they think someone killed Aunt Sis. Most of all, they believe I did it. You know why?"

"No, you tell me why."

"Because I did. I did it, and they have some evidence, or someone told them I should be a suspect. I never kept hating her a secret."

"Okay." Calley's tone suggested he didn't believe a word of it. "Go ahead and tell me how you did it. I'll listen, and believe me, I'll be the last person to pass judgment on you. I have good reason for saying that, but I'm not going to tell you what it is."

"Alright. When Aunt Sis went to the doctor for her chest pains, they gave her a bunch of medicine and vitamins to take. I knew she was dosing herself with home remedies and over-the-counter stuff, so I decided to add to it. I didn't know how much it would take to kill her. I don't know that's what I really had in mind. I just wanted to hurry her along a little.

"Anyway, I put foxglove in her vitamin capsules. I dumped out what was in there and filled them with foxglove. I figure she got along pretty well, but it gradually speeded up her heart until it finally gave out."

Calley frowned. "What are you going to do? If what you're saying is what really happened, they'll eventually arrest you."

"Oh, it really happened, all right. But I'm not going to confess. I'm going to see if they can come up with anything. I'm not going to run. That would make them all the more suspicious. I'm going to stick around and stick it out."

"You think that'll work?"

"Yeah. I feel I'm guilty like O.J. Simpson was guilty of killing his wife and her boyfriend. Neither of us is really guilty of murder. We killed people who deserved it. O.J. and me are just victims of a messed-up justice system that don't see things our way. O.J. got off on a technicality, and maybe I will too. Karma."

Calley said, "I guess if we all paid for our crimes, a lot more of us would be in prison. I don't figure anyone really gets away with anything, though. Karma collects in the end. Things balance out eventually, or the whole world would be a mess."

"I expect the Kennedys could write volumes on that one," said Devey.

Chapter 25

It seemed only a week, but it must have been longer. Calley and Lenya were grooming the lawn and Devey was doing dishes. Once again, Barry Pipare's Crown Vic appeared in the driveway.

Oh, shit, thought Calley. Barry is here to arrest Devey. They've found some evidence and the game is up.

Barry got out of the car and straightened his men-in-black suit, adjusted shades he must have swiped from a men in black movie, and walked toward the trailer.

"Official call or social visit?" asked Lenya.

"Official," Barry said bluntly. Avoiding further conversation, he walked toward the trailer. "Is Devey inside?"

Without waiting for an answer, he knocked on the doorjamb. Devey didn't seem at all surprised, and greeted him as she would greet a friend who came to call.

"I got news about your Aunt Sis's murder," he announced.

Calley felt his heart sink and steeled himself.

"Let's go in and sit down. The same news is good and bad."

They had suspected her all along, he said. In fact, he was

almost certain she was responsible for her aunt's death. "I was sure you'd laced her vitamins with rat poison. Brodifacoum. It's an anticoagulant they use now instead of warfarin. Causes internal bleeding and eventually death. That's what they found during the organ analysis phase of the autopsy anyway. Here's the good part, you're off the hook."

Devey's eyes widened. "Huh? You just said that you thought I killed her."

"Well, I would still think you did except that your daddy confessed to killing her for an insurance policy. When she moved in, she named him beneficiary. That policy was our first clue that he might have done it. He would have inherited the insurance money, but that was a drop in the bucket compared to what she had invested. She put money away like a pack rat for years. Made out like a bandit when the dot-com thing hit back in the late '90s. It's worth over two million, maybe three now."

"So who gets the money?" asked Lenya.

"You're looking at her. Your friend here," said Barry. "If she keeps it invested and lives off the interest, she won't have to work another day."

Devey, for all her sociopathic tendencies, felt badly about her father, and secretly felt the money wasn't hers at all. She would have killed Aunt Sis, and in fact, what she did may have contributed to an earlier demise. It was completely bizarre how this had worked out. She suddenly felt closer to her father than ever before and decided he would have the best lawyers, and who knows, maybe it could turn out for the best.

Barry stayed to explain some details Devey had to deal with now as well as how the case would probably go forward. Lenya and Calley asked him to stay for coffee and donuts.

"Calley, you know where a couple of old friends might go to

have that drink we talked about earlier?"

"Not within twenty miles of here," Lenya said. "Gibsonton is dry as a bone."

"Twenty miles doesn't sound far," Barry said. "I can burn some road in the Crown Vic and don't have to worry about tickets. You up for one hell of a ride, Calley? We'll get back in time for me to tell Devey what she'll have to do next."

"Okay, but I've got something I want you to do for me. I'll explain on the way."

Chapter 26

They barely made it to the two-lane when Calley began. "You're a state investigator, right? You're not just some errand boy for the law?"

"Hey, Calley. I may not be a TV detective, but I'm working on it. I do a lot of shit work now, but I'm on my way up."

"No disrespect, Barry. But I need to know if you got the juice to answer a funny question. You might have to bend some rules to get at what I want to know."

"So what're you up to, Calley? If it's about your girlfriend, she's taken care of. Her old man's taking the rap, and now he can't back out. Only thing that could go down bad is if your little girl finds a conscience and confesses to something more sinister."

"It's not Devey. It's Gibsonton. Weird vibes, like it's run by some kind'a dark force."

"So what? Why would I tell you about the place, even if I knew?"

"'Cause we're friends. And friends don't have to threaten friends with secrets they know," Calley said.

"And just what does that mean? What do you think you know?"

"I said friends shouldn't have to threaten friends with what they know. However, I seem to recall a few years back...what was her name...Mary Lou somebody ..." Calley chuckled.

"OK, so that's how it is. No threats, just drop a few career-ending words to the right people—take it to that newspaper gal you know, uh?"

"Wouldn't think of it."

"Okay, if that's what it takes to keep your ass quiet about Mary Lou. But know this—if you start blabbing, I'll have to kill you." Barry looked intently at Calley and didn't break a grin.

Calley exploded laughing and slapped Barry on the shoulder. But Barry grabbed his hand and tossed it back. Barry's dark eyes drilled through Calley. "It's not funny. Get this straight. Everybody on the force knows something's kinky about that place, but only a few know anything about what's really going on. I doubt anyone knows the whole story, even me. Whatever I tell you is for your ears only. If it gets out, you'll disappear forever. I don't really want to take you out Calley, but it's something I might have to do. If I don't do it, there are those who will. And, if I don't do it, they'll hit both of us. If they miss, they'll follow either of us to the ends of the earth. Now do you really want to know?"

"Holy shit! You aren't kidding, are you? Maybe I don't want to know after all. I was just curious, man, that's all. I'll back off. Whoa, calm down man."

"Curiosity killed the cat. You have no idea what you're messing with, man. I made a decision a few moments ago. For you it'll be one of those decisions that are irrevocable, one that's impossible to relive or to turn back for a different outcome. You know, I suppose I've wanted to tell someone about it all along. Then along came the perfect sucker, you, a guy who is asking for it. It'll be my perfect revenge for you threatening me about Mary Lou, White Girl, the Senator's daughter."

Chapter 27

Neither Leon Riluttante nor Lenya needed a car much. If Lenya bought a car, it had to be modified for her stature, and she would seldom use it anyway. She finally bought one because Leon agreed to chauffer her in exchange for the use of it. Essentially, it was a gift to Leon, because, except for an occasional visit to her doctor, Lenya seldom went anywhere.

"They've been gone a long time," said Devey.

"An hour to get there, an hour back, an hour at the bar. I figure about three hours," said Lenya. "Of course, the hour at the bar might stretch out."

"I'll have to go a bunch of places, said Devey. "Do you know anyone who has a car?"

"Well..." Lenya explained her arrangement with Leon.

"If he gets pissy about it, I'll pull rank on him and ask to see his registration. Hell, I even pay the insurance and inspections. Leon won't mind. It's early. Why don't we go see if he's agreeable?"

Devey grumbled, "If those two don't get back tonight, I may just take off in the morning by myself."

When they arrived at Leon's, Devey noticed the flagpole in his yard for the first time. It was tall enough, but the proportion wasn't right. And there was no flag.

"Is that what I think it is?"

"Yep. That's what's left of the swaypole that killed his wife. How'd you like to come home to that sucker every day? It gives me the willies, but Leon says he takes some measure of comfort in knowing it's out there. Sort'a like a tombstone, I guess. Wouldn't want one in my back yard though."

The two women climbed the steps to Leon's porch and Lenya hand-slapped the metal door. "Watch what you say," she cautioned, "Remember he ain't wrapped too tight."

Leon answered the door wearing a silk robe and, it appeared, not much else. It also appeared as if he'd been drinking.

"Hi Lenya, Who you got with you?" he said.

"That's Devey, you remember her. She was up here with her husband the other day. You met both of them."

"Oh yes, yes, yes, I remember now."

Leon began a long inquisition about the Crown Victoria he'd seen at Lenya's. It had to be some government agent or mobster. Only they drove such cars. He ruled out the Mafia because they drive Town Cars if they're cheap, or Caddies or Mercedes if they're rich. He was sure it was a government man because he dressed like a Man In Black. "Those shades are a dead giveaway, so why do they wear them? And, and they always talk into their wrist, what's with that?" he asked.

"They wear black shades so they can watch..." Devey felt a tug on her sleeve and dropped the conversation.

"Leon, listen," Lenya began. "We need the car for a few days..."

"I know what they're after! They ain't going to find it either,

I'll guarantee you!"

"What's that, Leon? What are they after?" asked Devey.

"Oh, no! Not so fast! Don't you wish you knew! Old Leon ain't that dumb to go off tellin' everybody what he knows. I'd have every MIB in the country up my ass if I was to even give you a hint."

"MIB?" Devey looked to Lenya.

"Men In Black," Lenya mouthed back.

"Oh," exclaimed Devey. "Have you ever seen any black helicopters? They say there's a lot of them flying around—"

Devey felt a sharp pinch and a pull on her arm. Lenya hissed, "Shut the hell up! Don't start that shit or we'll be here all day!"

Then, to Leon, she quickly added "Leon, honey, we won't tell a soul we were here. We'll not let on a thing to the man in the Crown Vic. We'll just take the car down to my place, if that's okay."

Leon looked at them suspiciously and foggily said; "You won't tell him what I got up here, will you?"

"No, Leon. I promise, I won't tell him a thing. I won't even mention I saw you. How's that?"

He pleaded with Devey. "You ain't seen any of them black choppers, have you?"

As they left, Devey asked Lenya what on earth Leon had that the government would care about.

"Damned if I know," said Lenya. "The guy's got more threads stripped than a left-handed nut on a road wagon. I'm glad I don't know much about him or his secrets. I figure most of them are in his head. You know, he gave me an overnight bag to keep for him. Said it was too dangerous to keep it at his place. I looked inside before I stuck it away. It was just a beat up old shopping bag with papers and a book in it. I never looked too close. I don't want to know. I'll bet it's nothing, but if it makes him feel good for me to keep it, I'll oblige him."

Chapter 28

Barry and Calley never did visit a bar or have the drink they had talked about. Instead, Barry drove slowly in silence for several miles.

"Well?" said Calley.

"I'm trying to think," he said. "I don't dare go anywhere close to Gibsonton. There's a good chance that everything for miles around is wired, or under surveillance of some kind."

"Even Lenya's doublewide?"

"Yes, most assuredly her doublewide. Okay, it sounds paranoid, but even the paranoiac has his enemies. This whole thing is in deep cover, and it just about runs through any State or Federal agency you can name. Lots of folks know about its existence but not many know why it's here. Most of us try to forget it," he explained.

"West Virginia isn't the bucolic state it appears to be on the surface. A long line of politicians have worked behind the scenes, cultivating the hick image while making the Mountain State a veritable rat's nest of high tech clandestine projects. If you think about it at all, West Virginia is the center of the personal identification universe.

"Over in the eastern part of the state at Green Bank, huge radio telescopes scan the skies and a few miles away Etam Earth Station keeps track of satellites, space missions, and some say eavesdropping on world-wide communications. Not too far from that, in the middle of nowhere with no seashore in sight and no hope of an ocean, there's a Naval Station.

"In Clarksburg there's a huge FBI Identification Center, and it's not just fingerprints anymore, it's biometric ID. The IRS has a huge data processing facility in Martinsburg—all information on anyone. Social security numbers, financials, all that stuff. Any agency with that sort of clout has the ability to conduct surveillance as well. The government has spent massive amounts in West Virginia just on its ability to keep track of people.

"In Fairmont, there's a NASA research center as well as a NASA technology center in Wheeling. All around the state are projects and buildings that are being built. When someone asks local residents about them, they don't seem to be aware of them at all.

"I'm going to tell you enough to get you hooked, but most of it is from scuttlebutt around the campfire at work. It's more of the 'they-said' variety. It's impossible to get verification on a lot of this, and anyone poking around will attract attention in a heartbeat. Attract too much attention and you disappear," said Pipare. "It's serious shit. You have to know that now you've attracted the interest of the people I work for.

"Remember all those people who died during the Clinton administration? Remember how it was just all—all—circumstantial" he didn't finish the thought. If Monica hadn't saved that dress, she'd be playing second chair harp behind Vince Foster right now."

He explained that the idea goes back to the Civil War. After the Lincoln assassination there was a lot of covering up to do and a bunch of spies and conspirators to take care of. Back then, there was plenty of space and folks could be shuffled off into a sort of witness protection thing. A guy who had served his country, but gained the enmity of his fellow citizens could go off to Arizona, establish a new identity, and live out his life, pretty much worry-free. Once out on the frontier, no one thought much about keeping tabs on any of them. It was a different world.

"After WWII things changed significantly. The Cold War increased a need for the sort of thing we're talking about," Pipare said. "Vietnam helped it along, and 9/11 blew it all to hell and gone. Now it's global in scope, and Gibsonton is only one cog in a big machine."

"So it's a hideout for sleazeballs who want to disappear?" said Calley.

"Not so fast, my man. There's more to it than that."

Pipare explained that taking care of sensitive witnesses was only part of the program. Given the current world political climate there're all sorts of people who need to disappear, some for an entire lifetime and some for a short while.

"Wouldn't just having them live out in the open, so to speak, be dangerous? Hell, Devey and I walked right into the place and looked around to our hearts content. No one except the gatekeeper said more than a couple of words to us. We were welcomed with open arms," Calley said.

"Calley, my man," Pipare said, touching Calley's leg, "remember this is West Virginia, where nothing is what it seems. Gibtown is made to be what it seems and what it seems, it's not. Both you and Devey are now on their list, in their databases, names occupations, bank accounts, fingerprints, pictures, and detailed personal histories. They probably have DNA samples by now. How do you think I found Devey so quickly with her hiding out in the middle of nowhere?"

"Well, what kind of dodge are they running then?" Calley asked.

"It's all about hiding in plain sight."

The dodge Barry was referring to began for Gibsonton sometime in the late 50's, around the same time the Eisenhower administration was planning the Greenbrier, a bomb shelter for Congress. Perhaps the same secret firms and contractors were involved in the Carnival Project as well.

Initially Project Carnival was intended for Cold War spies or diplomats who needed to "reorganize their lives." Now anyone of almost any stripe or nationality might be accommodated, depending on how important they are to U.S. Government interests, how much clout or money they have and what sort of contributions they are willing to make.

"The program began by initially soliciting government employees or their family members, but even that changed with time," Pipare said.

"Hell, all of 'em have their names out there on mailboxes or on their lawns. They don't appear to me to be hiding out to me unless, as you say, they're hiding in plain sight," protested Calley.

"That's the point. Ain't nobody hiding. Everybody's out in the open. That's how it works. That's the beauty of it."

He explained that government workers were ideal subjects for Project Carnival. They're often people who are looking for cradle to the grave care, not necessarily hard work; recently, more and more of 'em. Many of them will make almost any sacrifice to live a carefree life. The human resources files are full of this sort of unresourceful person, and the project managers were culling the databases for them. "Hell, you know as well as I do that the federal government has an unending supply of subjects who are looking for a free ride. They simply approached one of them with a questionnaire, they ask them if they'd like to volunteer for a safe assignment that would result in a life on easy street. Few of them who are ultimately chosen ever say no. And believe me, the chances of making the final cut are as likely as winning a Powerball drawing."

"I still don't think I get it," said Calley.

"If a person 'disappears' or is 'killed', or 'dies' of natural causes, it tends to make for problems. They are never going to live the good life if they have to live it as a dead or missing person. You know, travel, go to a Broadway play, dine out, or whatever," Barry said.

"I don't see how living a life, no matter how easy, in Gib-town in nowhere West Virginia is going to cut it for the sort of high rollers we're talking about," said Calley

"You forget, my man, nothing is what it seems in Gibsonton. The folks living there are the government employees who want to retire with full pensions, medical care, paid housing, paid transportation, month-long holidays, you name it. The folks who are 'disappearing,' 'dying,' being kidnapped or whatever replace those who move into Gibtown," he explained

"You mean—?"

"That's right. Let's say you are a dictator in a small country. The United States wants you out of the way, and you want to get out before the assassins hit. You call the embassy, arrangements are made. You dye your hair, get a facelift, or whatever, and you look a little like Joe Average Shmoe. Joe gets fitted for a house in Gibtown along with his wife, maybe even some family. Meanwhile, Jose Bonnano, the dictator, gets fitted for Joe's life," Pipare explained.

"Joe doesn't have to look much like Jose because Joe gets moved up in the world to a new position, but instead, he moves to Gibtown, then Jose fills his new position. They look enough alike and are similar enough to exchange passports, legal documents and with a little doctoring of both men and their papers the switch is complete."

"You mean all those folks in Gibsonton are the alter egos of—of—hell, I don't know what. You mean we've been living beside assassins, spies, Mafia dons and—"

"You're getting it buddy," said Barry as he slapped Calley on the shoulder. "But, you don't live beside them, you live beside the government workers who took their place. At our next little get-together, I'll let you in on some of the names and a little secret, even for Gibtown."

The black Crown Vic once more drove up the drive toward Lenya's home. Devey and Lenya were sitting on the deck absorbing the last rays of a setting sun. As Barry and Calley got out of the car, they walked to the deck, and without a word all of them moved toward the door.

Inside, Lenya poured coffee and served cookies as they talked about anything but the conversation between the two men. Barry announced that he would have to get a move on if he was to make it back to Charleston at a decent hour. Lenya offered him a night on the sofa, but he protested. The protest was obviously phony and Barry took off his shoes as Lenya and Devey spread blankets on the sofa.

While sleeping arrangements were made, Barry sat down with Devey and told her what she should do in the next few days. Devey made voluminous notes thinking all the while that there was no way she would ever accomplish everything Pipare told her. She only wanted to talk with her father and make sure he would have an easy time of it.

She would always wonder if he had been taking some of the stuff she put in Aunt Sis's vitamin capsules. Although she was prepared to spend days sorting out the events surrounding Sis's death, she would never spend more than a few hours in Grantsville and a few more in Madison, settling Siobhan Keavy's estate. It was a relatively simple matter since Sis had no outstanding debts and Devey was the only heir. There were a few bills to be paid here and there and a lawyer to be settled with after her inheritance was deposited in her new bank account. All of the expenses were taken care of by way of a loan from a family friend who knew he would collect when the insurance was paid off and some stocks were liquidated.

The next day, Pipare and Calley said their goodbyes in the relative privacy of Lenya's driveway. Barry sat in the driver's seat as Calley leaned in. "Buddy, I have no idea why you dumped all that shit on me. What makes you think I can keep my mouth shut anyway?"

"It doesn't matter much, does it?" Barry said.

"What do you mean?"

"I don't think you'll live that much longer anyway. I don't figure I will either," he added as almost an afterthought as he put the Crown Vic in gear and headed down the drive toward Charleston, or wherever he was going.

Devey borrowed Lenya and Leon's car anticipating she and Calley would be traveling back and forth between Charleston and Gibtown several times before things got back to normal— whatever that was. Things never seemed to turn out the way anyone expects.

Chapter 29

An American-born Sicilian of the new Coso Nostra, a wise-guy out of New Jersey, selected Johnny "Stomper" Stampanato and Louis "The Lout" Del Vecchio for the job. Stomper got his name from his first job. He wasn't satisfied to simply slit the guy's throat, Johnny stomped Paolo Pettalozzi to finish him off. "He was still squirmin'," said the Stomper. "No need in gettin' messy or wastin' good ammo. "What? You gotta problem wit dat?"

Johnny fancied himself a ladies man. He combed his hair back in a way that hasn't been in style since Vaseline Hair Tonic. He wore a suit that was just this side of zoot and patent leather shoes that looked like they had been discarded by a Damon Runyon character.

Louis wasn't as bright and performed the heavy lifting, much as a day laborer might view his job. For The Lout, a .22 caliber concealed in one hand was more than enough to assure a job was carried out. It was neat, quick and deadly. "Twenny two behind da' ear s'all ya' need. Not much blood, even takes a hard lookin' doc ta' find 'em sometimes. Spins aroun' ina' skull, scramles the braimz, nuthin' to it. Not much mess either," claimed The Lout.

His appearance belied his demeanor. He was dumpy and had a round face and close-set piggy blue eyes. A flat nose reminded one of a hog heading up the ramp in a slaughterhouse. It was about as aware of itself and its future as was Louis.

They arrived under cover of darkness. A quiet engine, parking lights and a moonless night and arrangements with ME assured no one would interrupt the job they were about to do.

"What'd dis guy do we gotta' wack 'im?" asked Louie.

"Don't know, don't care. My main job is not knowing anything. I get the guy's name; I arrange to do 'im, that's all I know, that's all I care. You know too much in this business, you wind up like your mark."

Louis continued to complain about how weird the place was. He noticed that the gatekeeper had waved them through with a big smile and it was as if they were being invited in for the evening.

"Boss says not to worry about security. Somehow they know we're expected, and they know no one is supposed to interfere. He says we're to use an icepick in the ear so's we don't leave no bloody mess to clean up. I'll put a rag over it until the bleedin' stops. They already got someone lined up for the house, an' house cleanin' ain't in the deal," said Johnny.

"It's awful dark. How we gonna' find the place?"

"It's right up ahead. Nicoletti, see the sign in da yard. It says NICOLETTI."

"Where you get an icepick? Ain't those hard to find nowadays?" asked Louie.

"Antique shop in Jersey. South Shore."

The two men cased the house and saw Mr. Nicoletti, formerly known as Mr. Muldoon, sitting under a floor lamp reading. He fit the description of the man they were to kill. Not Italian nor Sicilian, but an Irish redhead.

"We got the right town, the right place, the right man as far as I'm concerned. You wanna' do it or should I?" asked Johnny.

"When we get in I'll grab his arms and hold him down. You put the rag over his mouth for a gag and poke him with the pick. I'll use the rag, and you can sit on him until he stops jerkin' n' wigglin', and we'll get out of here and head for Clarksburg, catch our plane at Benedum, and be back in the city before morning,"

The two went to a side door. Johnny took a key from his pocket, and quietly put it in the lock, and opened the door. The two slipped inside and crept down the hall to the living room.

Johnny quietly slipped behind Mr. Nicoletti, and while Louis grabbed and held his arms, Johnny stuffed the rag in his mouth. Nicoletti struggled and lurched, but Johnny held tight and slipped the icepick into his right ear. He felt a slight crunch, then some resistance. He hit the handle a good shot, and Nicoletti went almost immediately limp. To be sure, he wiggled the handle around so that the hemorrhage would be massive and complete. He lurched and struggled a few seconds, then completely relaxed. The resulting smell of a loosened sphincter was overpowering.

Louie straightened the room as Johnny made sure whatever bleeding had stopped, and the wound was wiped clean. When they left, it was as if no one had been there. So far as Gibtown and its citizens were concerned, they were never there.

Mr. Nicoletti, it was reported, had died of a massive brain hemorrhage. He had no close relatives nor family so ME made the funeral arrangements. Mr. Nicoletti was packed into an ME ambulance/emergency car and hauled off to a crematorium in Charleston. The house was vacuumed, dusted and the curtains cleaned. When Mr. and Mrs. Rahdeep Patel moved in, they remarked that it really seemed like home. "Could you run the deodorizer a little longer, smells like somebody farted in here," said Mr. Patel.

"Got new neighbors over where Nicoletti lived," said the store clerk. "You know he died of a brain hemorrhage? Funny, though, they look more like feather Indians than dot Indians."

"Whatcha' mean dot Indians?" asked a customer.

"Red dot, right in the middle of the forehead. Not all of 'em though. Some of 'em got a turban and beard. Name's usually Singh though."

"Oh. You dumb shit, that ain't nice."

Chapter 30

Devey and Calley had just returned from an overnight trip to Charleston and were in the middle of a late evening dinner. Lenya was busy putting the dishes away when they heard a commotion outside.

Calley went to the door to see if he could determine what was going on. About a hundred yards away Leon was standing on a low hill looking upward with outstretched arms. He was dressed in a white silk robe, screaming to the top of his lungs.

Between the screams and howls Calley could hear, "Take me now Lord, my journey is complete. Take me to be with you and my Lynette. If you don't take me now, I'm sure they'll come. I know they're coming to get me if you don't. Take me now, I'm ready."

"It's Leon out there screaming his head off," Calley said.

"What should we do? Poor man, he probably needs help," said Devey.

"Aw, hell, the first time he did that I called the gatekeeper over there, and he called the MEs and they raised such a fuss, I quit calling. He does that about every couple of weeks. He'll get tired and go to bed here shortly. He's harmless. Just ignore him if you can," advised Lenya. "I figure he's suffering because of his wife's death and God knows what other demons he's strugglin' with. Demon Rum, I figure, is one of them."

"I know he's nutty and all that, but if he keeps that shit up, I'll go up there and strangle him myself," threatened Calley.

"He spent some time in Sharpe's. That's the mental hospital down in Weston, but they wouldn't keep him long. Gave him a bottle of pills and sent him home. Said they'd only keep him if he was a danger to himself or anyone else," Lenya said.

"He may not be a danger to himself, but if he doesn't quiet down pretty soon, I'll be a danger to him. Who do you think they are?"

"Who knows? He's always raving about the FBI, CIA, Mafia, don't think he's included the IRS or ATF yet. Don't worry, he probably doesn't know they exist."

"The poor guy. Just the thought of his wife impaled on that thing he keeps in the yard is enough to drive me to distraction. I'll bet he has nightmares about her every night," offered Devey.

"He won't take his medicine. Says it makes him feel weird. I figure weird for him is not being crazy and crazy is what he's used to," said Lenya.

"That's why I never did dope. Afraid I'd wind up in the loony bin, or worse, wind up like him," said Devey.

As if he heard the threats, he quieted down, then silence. Leon Riluttante gave up on his efforts to contact the Lord, who evidently had no intention of taking him yet.

Chapter 31

Leon Riluttante didn't get along with most of the people of the back lot and didn't mesh with anyone at all in Gibsonton proper. The fact that he was certifiably crazy didn't lend to his social graces either. About the only folks he socialized with were people with no social graces for starters.

Joey Judd fit right into that category like a palmed pawn in a chess game. Leon and Joey only fit when both were willing. Leon knew Joey was a little prick, and Joey knew Leon was crazy as Colonel Kurtz and twice as paranoid. Each knew the other's social frailties and accepted them as a means of two malcontents making friends, more by invention and necessity than amity.

They got together once each week to play gin, checkers, Chinese checkers or at times, chess. The meetings usually began with an argument over which game would be featured for the evening.

"You want to play chess because you know it makes me crazy," began Leon.

"Crazier, Leon, crazier. You're already as daft as Al Gore. You even move up a notch to that loony John Kerry—thinking he could be president," offered Joey.

"George Bush couldn't even shine Al or John's shoes. The man's a complete numb nuts," said Leon.

"See? See? That just proves you're crazier than a bedbug, you freakin' commie Democrat bastard. It's a known fact that all Democrats are messed up in the head. Take a look at Chuck Schumer and that Barney Frank wacko."

Joey knew Leon was a died-in-the-wool knee-jerk Democrat, and even though Leon didn't know it, Joey was a registered Democrat, too. Joey was just prick enough to pull his political chain along party lines.

"Okay asshole, what are we going to play? I suggest we play gin," offered Joey.

"You want to play gin because you know I get confused about what cards are out," complained Leon.

"No, you mental giant, I want to play because you can at least keep up when we play gin. If we play chess, half the time you don't even know the difference between a white square and a black one."

The banter went on for another half-hour until one finally relented and agreed with the other. It didn't matter which game, but they eventually played gin.

After the gin game, which Joey won, the loser suggested a cigar and brandy to end the evening on a brighter note. He moved bottles back and forth in the kitchen cabinets looking for the brandy.

"Whyn't you clean this shithole out, Leon?" asked Joey from his perch up on a kitchen chair.

"It's clean. I clean every other day, spray everything with disinfectant, and vacuum and dust."

"You know what I mean. Get rid of all these papers and books and crap you got stored all over the place. This place catch fire, you'd never get out."

Joey was on one side of the kitchen table, and Leon found a dusty half-full brandy bottle and took a chair on the other side. He was on his second brandy when he suddenly asked Joey if he'd like to see something really interesting.

"No, I don't want to see that nasty growth on your elbow," he replied. "You should get that looked after. That hair growing out of that sucker makes it look like a seedbed for alien life forms."

"It's not that. That finally went away. It's something my Cousin Ramón handed down to me when he died," said Leon.

"The Cousin Ramón, the movie star you told me about? The Cuban revolutionary who escaped Castro's prisons and floated to Miami?"

"That's the one."

"You told me all about how he helped Castro take over Cuba. No wonder you're such a communist, pinko shit. Castro's the biggest dictator since Mussolini. And don't tell me how everything in Italy ran better when he was the dictator either," said Joey.

"This doesn't have anything to do with Castro. At least I don't think it does. It's something entirely different from that stuff," said Leon all too quietly.

"Leon, I really don't give a shit what your cousin left you, unless it's something I can eat, drink or smoke. I used to throw in something to screw, but those days are gone. If you want me to look it over, get it out here."

Leon left the kitchen table and went to his bedroom, cautioning Joey not to follow. In the bedroom he rummaged through drawers and cabinets until he found what he was looking for.

He brought out a manila envelope that looked brand new.

Joey said, "That doesn't look too old. I thought you said your cousin died years ago. That envelope looks like it just came from Office Depot."

Leon explained that the envelope was relatively new. He had taken the things he wanted to photocopy to Staples and made photocopies of them. He put all of the documents in a brand new ten by twelve envelope he purchased for the occasion.

"These aren't the originals," he said. "Only a few pages out of a book and a couple of letters or something. I put the whole thing—the originals—in good hands so if anyone would come looking for them, they'd be safe," said Leon.

"Who'd come looking for that shit? Don't tell me, I already know. The CIA, FBI, Mafia, ATF."

"What's the ATF?"

"Never mind. Do you know how all that CIA-Mafia stuff sounds Leon? It makes you sound like a raving lunatic. Oh, I forgot, you are a raving lunatic. You've got a great alibi, though. If anything bad goes down, you can always plead insanity, you insane asshole you. Any judge will believe it, and you got the entire community to back you up. Hell, I'll even testify."

"You're gonna' act like that, I'll just put 'em all back," Leon threatened.

"You know you're a bipolar, manic depressive, nutbar, para-noid screwball. That thing, that pole you got out in the yard, is a perfect metaphor for you. When you were on top, you were way up, manic as hell, swaying back and forth from delusion to delusion. When you got down, there you were trying to fig-ure some way to put yourself out of your misery."

"You know," said Leon, "I never thought of it that way, but you're right. One hundred percent correct. It's a stand-in for old Leon. I think you've got something there."

"Damn straight," affirmed Joey.

"If it wasn't for you, I'd be right down there at the bottom of that damned pole, diggin' myself a little hole to crawl into."

"See? See what friends are for? And you called me a prick. I'm the best friend you got."

"Don't go thinkin' you're doing me any a big favors. Having you around is a total distraction. I get so pissed off at you; I don't have time to think about what a miserable piece of shit my life is. In a way, Joey, if you weren't such a big pain in the ass, I might even be up there in heaven with Lynette now."

Joey considered asking him why in the world he would think Lynette Riluttante, the two-bit whore of the back lot would be doing in heaven, but he figured Leon was bombed enough now to even rise to the bait, or if he did, he'd beat the living crap out of him.

"You've given new meaning to my life, Leon," said Joey, "now I can be a miserable shit and asshole and still do something for someone. Just like that Starvation Army."

"Salvation, Joey, Salvation."

"I know, I know, I'm your salvation. Ain't I a prince?" exclaimed Joey.

"Aw, forget I said anything. You wanna' see my cousin's stuff or not?"

Chapter 32

In the old days Emilio "The Boss" Porrello would have been called a *capo di tutti capo*, but the old days were long gone. The tasks of thugs like Johnny Stampanato and Louis Del Vecchio were pretty much the same, but la Cosa Nostra wasn't. It was more like one of the corporations down in the financial district. In fact a major gripe among the old gang was the family had moved to a nuovo deco di arte office down there. Hell, you could see Trinity Church from the doorway. La vergogna, nessun orgoglio. There was no pride anymore. No more of the Godfather-style of wise guys. Joe Pesci had turned the image of wise guys into a stereotypical joke, but no one in the family was laughing.

Emilio sat behind his desk in a corner office. Johnny and Louis sat in a poshly decorated waiting room attended by an Eastern European looking matron.

"Hey—hey—Brunehilde. Hey, I'm talkin' to you," said Louis.

"The name's Zvonmira Draganja. My friends call me Zavon. You may call me Miss Draganja," she responded coolly.

"Well, ain't Miss Dragonbreath a pisser. I just wanted to

know how much longer we wuz gonna' have'ta wait," said Louis as the door opened and they were allowed to enter Emilio's office. Johnny would have liked to have stayed in the waiting room with Louis to see what would happen next, but duty called.

"Come in, come on in, gentlemen," invited Porrello.

Louis made a show of looking around and said, "I wuz just lookin' for those gents you wuz talkin' about."

Porrello squirmed in his seat and sighed.

"Just a joke. No harm intended; just a joke."

"Yes, Mr. Del Vecchio, very amusing. Please, both of you have a seat."

"I—" Johnny began.

Suddenly Mr. Porrello's nice side disappeared. He went right to work; and his first task was to intimidate.

"You don't have shit to say about anything, so shut up," Porrello shouted. "You, too, Mr. Del Vecchio. All I want to from you two are responses to any questions I have. I don't want hear either of you say a damned thing. Is that perfectly clear?"

There was a deafening silence.

"I said you could respond to my questions, you dumb shits."

"Yes, Mr. Porrello, we got it clear, we got it very clear," said Johnny, sheepishly.

"You fellas' done good on that Nicoletti job. Not a hitch. Gives me confidence I can trust you with this one, so don't screw it up."

"We aim to—" Johnny caught himself as he saw fire in Prorrello's eyes."

"Did I ask you a question?" he shouted."

"I—"

"I didn't ask you a damned thing, did I?" he screamed at Johnny.

Louis quivered in his seat.

Silence.

"Now, you dumb ass, I asked you a question."

"Huh?"

"I asked you if I asked you a freakin' question."

"Huh?"

"The answer, you dumb shit is NO!" The "NO" sounded like it was shot out of a cannon.

"Now, boys, let's see if we can all get on the same page here. The man has a job that needs done. I told him I had a couple of guys who could pull it off without too much trouble. Now are you those guys, the kind who can do that?"

"I ain't sayin' shit," mumbled Louis.

"Did you say something, Mr. Loo-ee?" asked Porrello sarcastically.

Louis pointed to himself and barely got out, "Me? Ah, no, musta' been the air-conditioner, I didn't say nuthin'"

"Well?" said Porrello.

Johnny, feeling confident that a question he could answer was now before them, said, "We're your guys. You tell us who you want done and we'll do him. We'll do him without a ripple. You can depend on it."

Louis now felt more like talking. "Yeah, we're the guys."

"Okay, Okay, enough. Now keep your mouths shut until I tell you what has to be done. After I get through, you can ask all the questions you want. This one ain't easy. It's going to be right out in the open for everyone to see."

"Ain't that damned near impossible?" asked Louie.

"Hey, I'm hiring experts. You guys are supposed to be smart, you figure out how you're going to do it. No one said it was going to be easy. The man wants it done a certain way."

The rented Mercedes hummed along a back road with Johnny Stampanato at the wheel. Typically he'd let Louis drive, but he felt he thought more clearly, more creatively when he was driving.

It must have been nearly 9:00 in the evening because it was nearly dark. A moonless night would soon overtake the long shadows of the afternoon and the car would be enveloped in blackness.

"How we gonna do this thing Johnny?" Louis began.

"I'm thinkin, I'm thinkin, or can't you tell? Why don't you try it a while? It'll be a new experience for you. I'm just going to sit here and drive and wait for you to come up with some kind of plan," challenged Johnny.

They drove on in silence and were nearly to the interstate when Louis moaned and mumbled something.

"What?" said Johnny.

"This kind of thinkin, it makes my brain hurt. I'm tryin', I'm tryin' real hard, but nuthin' comes out. I just go around in circles…and…and nuthin'. I'm just not used to doin' this. It's hard."

"I been thinking while you were tryin' to think, ya' know?"

"Yeah, you come up with anything?" said Louis.

Johnny explained how the job had to happen. It was going to have to be in broad daylight, for everyone to see so it would be a warning to the residents of Gibtown and its suburbs. It wasn't going to be another accident or medical mishap that caused the death of one of the residents this time. After The Stomper and The Lout were through, the fear of God would be in the forefront of everyone's mind.

Johnny began to lay out his plan. He wanted to bounce it off of Louis so that if there were any real flaws in it, he might just be bright enough to point them out.

The plan was to burn the guy's home. It had to be a flash fire that enveloped the whole thing, but a fire that would endure long enough to render everything to ashes. The proposed victim's body couldn't be in the fire. It had to be not only found; it had to be on public display until the coroner arrived. In Gibtown's part of the world that would be the least of their problems. It might take all day for the coroner to get there.

"I ain't never been no torch," exclaimed Louis. "I ain't against it, understan, I just ain't never did it before."

"You can handle that part. I'll tell you everything you have to do. I'll handle the guy we gotta' wack. He's old and shouldn't be any trouble at all," said Johnny.

Johnny explained to him that the accelerant would be gasoline along with some motor oil mixed in to thicken it up a little. Next they would mix in another ingredient to make it gooey so it would stick to everything.

"The stuff is just like napalm," Johnny explained. "You slosh it everywhere. Might even take a mop and put it up the walls. To keep the fire going, we'll set some buckets of kerosene around. They'll light up, but burn slower."

"Do I get to light er up?" asked Louis.

"If you're that freakin' dumb, I should let you. NO dumb-ass. That shit's gonna' blow. We have to make sure all the windows and doors are open. We want to double-check that. If it blows up it'll take the whole neighbor-hood.

"I know where I can get a gizmo that you can call on a walkie-talkie, and when it gets the signal, it shoots out a hell of a spark. Our asses will be down the road a mile or two before we set it off. It should be put near one of the buckets of kerosene so it burns up in the fire. Leaving the body there to be found is the only clue we're leaving behind."

"Sounds like you know what you're doin' to me," Louis assured him.

Chapter 33

Lenya, Devey and Calley were on the front deck when it started this time. At first Devey said she thought it was Leon out baying at the moon again, but then they heard a voice that sounded like it was coming from the Mayor of The Munchkin City. At that point everyone knew it was Joey Judd.

"They're at it again," said Lenya. "I don't know why one of them puts up with the other. Joey goes over there at least once a week to play cards and they get into it. Sounds like a Great Dane trying to screw a Chihuahua."

"Sounds like they're hung up," Calley offered with a laugh.

The arguing went on for about a half-hour and then quieted down except for periodic flare-ups. At about 11:00 there was a major argument along with noise in the form of slamming doors, then silence. Lenya, Devey and Calley assumed the game had broken up for the night or the game had broken them up.

No one suggested that anyone check to see if Joey had killed Leon or vice-versa. In the past when anyone checked, they found a few scrapes and bruises and one time a bitten ear, but neither of them had killed the other—yet.

"Did you notice that Leon, or someone, had planted flowers around that pole?" said Lenya.

"Yeah," said Calley. "That kind of worries me."

"Why?" asked Devey.

"As many times as Leon has threatened to do himself in, I fully expect to go out there some morning and find him hanging from it."

Lenya assured them that she thought that was a remote possibility. "He's been living here since I came and he's threatened to join Lynette just about every week or so in all that time. If he was going to do it, he'd have done it already by now. Between you and me—and believe me, I never tell him this—I don't think he has the nerve. It would be like him going out and climbing that pole again to perform on top. It just ain't in him no more. I don't think he'll kill himself; he just ain't got the guts. And, being Catholic, he believes if he kills himself, he won't get to heaven and be with his precious Lynette."

"You never know," said Devey. "The myth is, those who say they're going to, never do. But I suppose you can also subscribe to the fact 'they say' if someone is determined to do it, they'll find a way. I'm with Calley, I don't like the new garden and I don't like that pole standing out there. It creeps me out."

"Speaking of death and dying, did you hear about the guy over there in town who died last week?" said Calley. "There was so much going on around here that we barely noticed it."

"Could we talk about something a little more pleasant? This conversation has turned to the morbid side," said Lenya.

"I know, I know, but there's something weird about it. The guy at the store says it's the third brain hemorrhage they've had in two years. Says he thinks there may be something in the water or the pesticides they use to kill roaches in the houses."

"Calley, if there's one thing I learned living here, it's don't ask about things that don't concern you. If ME's negligence is causing folks over there to die off, I'm sure they wouldn't be too pleased if folks started asking questions," cautioned Lenya. "As long as it stays behind their fence, I don't care if there's a shit hemorrhage or a brain hemorrhage a week."

Chapter 34

A week had passed since the last game Joey and Leon had played. Joey and Leon were masochists at heart so neither was certain who had set the schedule for the next game. Joey showed up and assured Leon he had invited him over for something.

They traded the usual insults without incident and, with no basis for an argument, decided to play checkers. There was a brief tiff when Joey decided on his own that jumps were optional and that he should be able to avoid multiple captures of his men by not jumping into a trap Leon had set for him.

"If you don't have to jump me, there ain't no game to it. This shit could go on forever. Now jump me," Leon told Joey.

"What do you do, make up the rules as we go along? It don't say nowhere that I gotta' jump you," Joey declared.

"You want rules, I'll show you rules," said Leon, who abruptly jumped up and started rummaging through drawers, cabinets and stacks of papers. He finally came up with a book titled Win at Checkers, which he waved in Joey's face. He also found the envelope that contained photocopies of the material from his Cousin Ramón.

"Ah ha," exclaimed Joey, "you been cheatin'. You been reading up on how to play so you can beat me. You beat me, what's it prove? I'm not that smart, so you're not smarter, and you're still an insane, paranoid schmuck."

"I don't wanna' play no more," said Leon. "Look, I found that stuff we were going to look at the other night. Let's look through it an see if we can figure out what it's all about."

"What the hell do you mean, 'what it's all about?'"

"Joey, I've had this stuff for quite a while and I still don't know what it is. My cousin said it was important and the government, Men In Black, CIA or Mafia wanted it. He said they'd do anything to get it too. You're my friend. You help me figure it out," Leon pleaded.

"You know what I figure? I figure your cousin was as crazy as a cockroach too. I think it runs in the family, congenital idiots—that's what I think."

"You know what I think, Joey? I think you think I won't kick the shit out of you because you're a little twerp midget, that's what I think."

"That did it. You know how pissed off I got the last time you used the 'M' word. That did it. Now you have to say you're sorry, and you'll never do it again."

Leon decided on the spot that it would be better to apologize than be convicted of murdering a little person. After all, he couldn't claim self-defense, so he told Joey he was sorry as he got out the envelope and spread the contents on the kitchen table.

"Say you'll never make fun of your little person friend again," Joey said.

"I'll never make fun of another little person again," Leon said.

Joey noticed the slight, but let it slide because he knew they would never get past it. To divert attention from the argument, he picked up one of the papers from the table and began to look it over intently, or at least he pretended to.

"Hey, Leon, what's this from?" he asked.

"I copied that from the book," Leon replied.

"It's got dates and days of the week in printing, then at each day it's got stuff written in long hand. Looks like the page of some kinda' diary or log to me. Musta had some days where more happened than others cause they wrote over top of some of the printing."

Joey pointed out that much of it was unreadable because water had gotten onto it and blurred the ink. Other parts were written in pencil and were smeared by wear, but those parts were more readable.

"Didja' copy anymore pages?"

Leon told him that he copied a couple more, but the whole book was a mess.

"What's this here? Looks like a will or something."

"Oh, that's just one of my suicide notes," Leon said as if he were talking about a laundry list. "I write those all the time, usually throw em away. Don't really have the nerve to do it, but I feel better after I write a few. Don't know how that got in there."

Leon told Joey that he could read some of the book. He would appreciate some outside help. He asked Joey if he could make out parts he couldn't decipher.

Working together, they agreed that one long passage was about a day that included someone, or something, named ATTGEN or ATYGEN and some kind of a game, they couldn't make out, but it looked like Black Jack. At the end of the page was a quote from someone "Fo ve you emies, but n rget the names."

"I figure that's 'Forgive your enemies, but never forget their names'," said Leon.

"You know, Leon, you amaze the shit outa' me. For being a nutcase, you figured that out all by yourself. Hell, Forrest Gump coulda' got that one."

"On this other page there's Black Jack again, and Bob and over here, there's that ATYGEN again and MoMo. Over here's something called the In-Law. And over here, the Chairman and the director. You know that quote sounds like Mafia shit to me. Remember what the Godfather said?"

"Yeah," said Leon. "'Keep your friends close, but your enemies closer,' *Godfather II*, 1974."

"Hey, you know your movies, but I don't think Michael Corleone was the first one that said it. Anyway that quote sounds exactly like sumthin' a mob boss would say."

"I think I know what it is," declared Leon abruptly. "It's as obvious as the nose on your face. I'll bet it's the minutes of meetings. The ATY is the attorney for the company and the chairman is chairing the meeting, or is the Chairman of the Board. MoMo was Sam Giancana's nickname and they were talking about gambling in Vegas—Black Jack. In-Law must be they were talking about gambling in Vegas, making something lawful. It all fits. The other names are people who were at the meeting or being talked about."

"Holy shit! I think you're onto something. That would explain why the government, FBI, CIA has been after it and it would also explain why the Mafia wants it. They want it back. Joey, you're a frigging genius," Leon proclaimed, slapping him on the back. "You know Frank Sinatra's nickname was The Chairman of the Board, and they say he was connected. I think you're onto something."

"Hey, this ain't so hard! I figured it out and, as crazy as you are, I think you were just looking for me to confirm what you knew all along. I just thought of something, though."

"What's that, Leon?"

"I dunno, maybe they was makin' a movie. That may be what they were talking about The Director. And you got all these Hollywood big shots. Anyway, I'm thinkin' if any of this stuff is such hot shit, what's to keep 'em from finding this thing?"

"I ain't got it, and the beauty of it is, the person who's got it don't know they got it. And you know what?"

"No, tell me what," Joey said.

"I'm giving these here copies to you. You can put 'em in a safe place 'cause you never know who might come looking for 'em."

"Thanks a whole pants-load, Leon, but no thanks. I got enough problems being a full-time little prick. I don't need no more problems."

"You'll do it. Just take 'em and hide 'em. I'll give you a hundred dollars if you do it. Just hide 'em away. No one but us will know, and I don't even want to know what you do with 'em. If you can't trust yourself, who can you trust?"

The money sealed the bargain for Joey, who was always in need of a few bucks. Leon's fate was sealed long ago when he took the book from Ramón Villavicencio.

"You know why they called Sam MoMo?" asked Joey. "It was a reference to Mooney, which is gangster talk for crazy. You see, Sam Giancana was a crazy mutha, just like you are," said Joey with a nervous, mirthless laugh that cross-faded off into another thought.

Chapter 35

Except for the periodic, predictable ravings of Leon and his fights with his friend Joey, life on the outskirts of Gibtown was idyllic. Devey and Calley hadn't found employment, but they worked around the doublewide doing light maintenance, housekeeping, and living from day to day. Lenya seemed to enjoy their company, and at the rate the couple's money was being spent, they could stay on for some time before they had to even touch the inheritance.

From time to time one or both of them went to the store in town, "over there," and a couple of times they drove the Lenya-Leon car to Charleston for a shopping safari. They never bought much because there wasn't much they needed.

Entertainment consisted of an occasional card game at the kitchen table, reading, and listening to the radio. They took long walks and, when the weather was nice, they all assembled on the front deck to watch the sun set and to listen for the still of the evening to set in.

One evening they were sitting on the deck after sunset. It had been a while since a Leon vs. Joey match, so they were attuned to the quiet of the night as it fell across the valley. A few chirping birds found their nests and cooed the dusk into night. It wasn't humid or muggy. The air was warm, but clear, and Lenya dozed in a recliner near the side of her trailer. Calley had taken a seat on a bench near the rail and was looking across the front lawn to the road beyond when Devey joined him and, linking her arm with his, snuggled beside him.

"That's funny," he said.

"What's funny?" asked Devey.

"A car going out this time in the evening. A big black car. You don't see those around here much."

"Probably someone just passing through," suggested Devey offhandedly.

"Maybe so. Looks like they're in a hurry though. Hope they don't bottom that thing out on one of those humps down by the corn field."

A moment of silence passed as the couple moved closer together, and Lenya began to snore. Except for her light snoring, there was a deathly quiet. No crickets, no katydids, just a firefly or two in at the edge of the tree line, not a sound.

Then suddenly, a heavy, distant thud and whoosh of air. Next a brief boom and several pops, then a brilliant glow that lit up the sky over toward Leon's place. At the top of the glow was a dense cloud of black smoke.

"Oh, Geeezus," said Lenya under her breath. "Leon's finally caught that firetrap he lives in on fire."

Calley and Devey had taken off their shoes, and Calley was frantically trying to put his back on.

"Stay here," he said to the women. "I'll go see if there's anything that can be done. "No use for you two going up there now and getting in the way of fire equipment. The ME Fire Department should be here pretty quickly."

As Calley topped the rise he could see the outline of what

was left of the trailer. What remained at this point wasn't much more than a few sticks in the air and melted aluminum. The small trailer looked as if it had been incinerated.

From the light of the glowing ruin, the swaypole memorial stood out in silhouette. From the rope that was meant to hold a flag at some future time, Leon was dangling by his neck. His feet were only inches from the ground and a nearby, upturned, kitchen chair. Leon, the chair, and the pole were charred from the intense heat.

After a few moments, the MEFD pickup arrived, but there was nothing to save. Anyone in the trailer would have been burned to a cinder. Any of Leon's belongings had suffered a similar fate. About the only things remaining were a few boards too wet to burn from the deck, the remains of the sway-pole, and the remains of Leon.

"These things go up like tinder. Nothing worse than a trailer fire. This one went faster than any I can remember," said one fireman to another.

The fire company hosed what embers remained and considered cutting Leon down. No one wanted to take the responsibility and absolutely no one wanted the job, so it was decided to leave Leon on display where he was until the coroner arrived.

Chapter 36

Much later that day, a hearse-like van drove up the road to Leon's former dwelling. It was met there by an ME utility truck. Two men got out of the truck, and one woman got out of the van.

Watching from a distance, Calley assumed the woman was the coroner or medical examiner who had driven from Charleston or Grantsville. Of course, it couldn't have been anyone else.

The crowd that had been hanging around most of the day disappeared quickly although a few stayed nearby, hoping to hear something, among them, Joey Judd, a figure who was hard to miss and a personality hard to ignore.

"I'm his friend. We played cards and checkers together," he said as he imposed himself on the woman who was now getting some equipment out of her van.

"That's nice," she said coolly. "I'm sure some of the investigators will want to talk with you, but for now, please stand over there out of the way."

Joey moved to the side of the driveway just as a black Crown Victoria arrived. It pulled in behind the van, and Barry

Pipare stepped out from behind the wheel.

"Next in line for the shit job?" said Marcia Broam, the pathologist.

"Just like you, huh?"

"Yep, not as exciting as a genuine crime scene investigator." She shot back. "Your job's not nearly as messy either."

The two knew each other from other investigations and each had an appreciation for the other's job. However, each of them knew they were both new troops, and they knew who got the Hicksville assignments.

"Can't say you don't know the drill around these parts," she said. "No one's interested in any theories, so we take what we see and report this thing the way it appears. Keeps everybody happy."

"Why? You got reason to think it's anything other than a suicide?" Pipare asked.

"Nope. I figure they sent you here to keep it low profile and, believe me, I'm not going to look any farther than the evidence in front of us indicates. I saw one of his buddies, a little munchkin fella', a few minutes ago. You might want to question him. I told him to get out of my hair. Said he used to play cards and checkers with the air dancer up there," she said, jerking a thumb in the direction of the hanging body.

"I'll tell the two ME guys over there to help cut him down. What's his name?" asked Pipare.

After referring to a clipboard, she said, "Says here it's Leon Riluttante. An ex-carny, came here when his wife was killed. They had some kind of aerial act. The rigging broke, and she was fatally injured. According to this he's been temperamental and despondent ever since. Pretty cut and dried, I'd say."

"I think you're right. I don't see any reason for mucking about trying to turn it into something. It would just piss everyone off if it becomes more than a suicide anyway," offered Barry.

"It's a shame no one cut him down," she said. "Guess he's a little taller now anyway."

"Yeah, everyone watches TV, and they know not to disturb the murder scene. Well, in this case a suicide scene, but you know what I mean."

The ME guys had lowered the body and were trying to figure a way to get it into a black bag when Marcia interrupted them.

"I want to take a quick look before you zip that up."

She made a cursory examination that confirmed her suspicion it was suicide. The men had left the noose around his neck. It was tied in a typical hangman's knot that every school kid, evidently including Leon, learns to tie.

While the ME boys put the body into the van, Marcia went over and picked up the charred chair.

"I figure he poured some gas or other accelerant in the trailer, set the dump on fire, and got up on that chair. Kicked it out from under him and took his last swing. Don't think it broke his neck though. Not enough drop. Probably just passed out, then passed on." she said to Barry.

"I'm going to see if I can find the little person you were talking to. Are you headed out now?" Barry asked.

"Yeah, gotta get back to the ranch and work this mess up before I end the day. I'll make sure you get a copy of the report."

"I appreciate that. I'd like to invite you for a drink sometime if you can keep the conversation away from our work."

"You got a deal," she said as she climbed into the van.

Chapter 37

Pipare had the odd feeling that he wasn't going to like anything that Joey Judd would have to tell him. His gut was telling him that there was more to this than met his eyes so far. If it was something that disagreed with what he and Marcia decided, he wasn't going to like it one bit, and he was sure his boss wouldn't like it at all.

It didn't take much effort to locate Joey. He hadn't gone far, and when Pipare heard his yammering and saw how tall he was, he was pretty sure he had his man.

"You Joey Judd?" Barry asked.

"That's what they call me. Who wants to know?"

"I have to ask you some questions. You got a problem with that?"

"Should I have an attorney present?" Joey asked sarcastically.

"Only if you think you need one." Pipare knew Joey was full of it because it would take a day or two to get an attorney to come out here. And it would take a lot of money that Joey didn't appear to have.

"Tell you what. Why don't you go back to your place, get

comfortable, have a drink of water and I'll stop by after I see some other people." His idea was to give Joey a chance to cool off and think things over for a while. Hopefully the little man would be more rational and helpful later. In the meantime he would call on his old friend Calley Crowcroft and his girlfriend, Devey.

Pipare found the three of them sitting on the deck and talking about how the day had unfolded. He coughed as he approached to make sure they wouldn't think he was slipping up on them.

"Hi there, Mr. Investigator. How's it going up there at the crime scene?" asked Calley.

"It's going. I had to take a break, so I thought I'd come down here and see you folks," he said.

"Think we have anything to add?" asked Devey.

"Don't know; do you, Calley? What makes you think it was a crime scene?"

"I suppose it was just a snide comment. Investigators are usually investigating murder. I suppose I should have said 'death scene,' to be perfectly and politically correct. Wouldn't want any family members to feel bad if I called it a suicide, which is what it is," said Calley defiantly.

"Come on now, pal, you don't know if it's anything but a death at this point. You got any information I don't?"

Calley only shrugged. He could see he wasn't going to make any points by telling him how ridiculous the whole thing was.

"It looks like a suicide, and that's probably what we're dealing with, but I'm going to cover my ass and ask some questions if you don't mind?" Barry reminded him.

Later, after Pipare thought enough time had elapsed for Joey to have cooled off and gained some composure, he went over to Joey's place to question him. After a brief introduction and a display of credentials that Joey insisted upon, Barry began his questioning.

"Hope you're not mad at me for insisting on seeing your credentials. I have my reputation of being a little prick to protect," Joey said with a big grin.

"Never hurts to know who you're talking with at a time like this," Barry said. "Now just go over your relationship with the deceased and tell me anything that comes to mind. If I have questions, I'll break in to ask."

Joey told Barry how he and Leon made it a practice to meet periodically to bitch at each other, play a game or two and generally shoot the shit. He also made it clear that he thought Leon was a nut case and, if things happened the way they should in this world, Leon would have been in a mental hospital and taken care of.

"It ain't right," Joey said. "It somehow just ain't right."

Joey said he held the opinion that it was the book that killed him. "Don't make no difference if he did it, or somebody else did it to him, the book is what did him in."

"What do you mean, the book?" asked Pipare.

Joey explained how Leon had inherited a book that he believed was being sought after by sinister forces of some kind. He told him he didn't think Leon knew what it was, but he had reason to believe some powerful people were after it.

When Pipare asked if he had any idea what the book was about, Joey told him about the time he and Leon had sat and tried to decipher the photocopies Leon had made. He explained that they both believed the book contained the minutes of the meetings of a Mafia family, and he told him how they had reached that conclusion.

"You still have the photocopies?" Pipare asked.

"I'm going to tell you and I'll swear to it under oath, I burned them, but yeah, I still got em. I figure they're worth a pretty penny, so I hid em away where nobody can find them."

"Don't worry, I won't tell anyone you have them. If Leon was killed because of something he knew, then you might be at risk as well. If you'll just show them to me, I'll take a quick look and give them right back," Pipare assured him.

Joey said he knew Barry and Calley were friendly, so he asked if Calley could be present when the documents were turned over. Calley could be a witness to the proceedings.

"It's not that I don't trust ya, understand. It's just that these things might be valuable, and I don't want 'em confiscated or something like that. You know how the government is when it comes to something valuable," cautioned Joey.

"You get the papers, and I'll be right back," said Pipare

Within a few minutes Barry returned with Calley. On the way over he explained to Calley that he was to witness the exchange and the return of some papers that Leon had given to Joey. He also cautioned Calley that the existence of the papers was to be kept an absolute secret.

When they reached Joey's home, he had the papers laid out on the kitchen table with the new manila envelope nearby. Pipare took out a magnifying glass and began to inspect one of the papers while Calley looked over a similar one.

"That one there and the one he's got are about the Mafia meeting," Joey declared as if it were fact.

"You mind if I make notes, Joey? I won't try to copy the papers or anything, I just want to have a future reference," said Barry.

"I—I—guess—not," he said hesitantly. "I don't think that would cause any harm. Don't mark on anything, though."

Barry wrote down ATYGEN, Black, Jack, Bob and the 'Forgive your enemies, but never forget their names' quote. After that he wrote MoMo, Chairman of the Board, In Law, Pres., Joe, and SS.

Joey, looking over Pipare's shoulder, explained how he and Leon had figured out that the book was minutes of Mafia meetings.

"I figure some important people would like to get their hands on that book. I know the government would like to have it. I bet it would clear up a lot of stuff that happened back then," said Joey.

Pipare mumbled something about how he might be right, but seemed to be deep in thought, trying to put the pieces of stained and obscured writing together.

Without saying another word, Barry gathered the papers and shoved them back into the envelope and handed them to Joey.

"You go and hide these where nobody can find them. I don't even want to have a clue where you put them. You can burn them if you want. I'm not advising you to do it, but if it was me, that's what I would do. As far as I'm concerned they don't exist, you got that?"

"Yes, sir," Joey said, now in awe of Pipare.

"What did you make of all that?" asked Calley as the pair walked back to Lenya's place.

"If I told you, I'd have to kill you," he said mirthlessly.

"Now don't start with that secret agent shit again," Calley warned.

"You know enough about Gibtown and some other stuff, so I know you can be trusted. I know you can be trusted because if a smell of this gets to the media or leaked to some other person, I can personally guarantee you'll be toast, just like Leon. That's not a threat, Calley. I won't even have to think about it. You'll have an accident, an aneurysm or commit suicide.

I don't know which, but the death certificate is already made out. It just needs a name put on it. Believe me when I say this is far more important than the Gibtown secrets."

Chapter 38

For whatever reason, a reason he could never figure out, Pipare wanted Calley to be present when he saw the papers. Perhaps it was because Calley was already in so deep and Pipare needed backup, Barry invited him to accompany him to a meeting in Elkins to discuss his findings with a man he knew as his boss, a man whose name he didn't know, and whose face he'd never seen. All Pipare knew about his boss was that he spoke with what he assumed was a south Texas drawl.

When he mentioned this to Calley, he asked him how they had meetings if he never saw him. Barry explained the boss was "behind a curtain thing, kind of like in the *Wizard of OZ*."

Upon hearing this, Calley almost soiled himself. This wouldn't be the last time he'd be brought to the Oz brink. Calley thought, this is freakin' la-la land, and this guy is taking me down the yellow brick road. His brain switched off or went out of gear as "We're off to see the Wizard" played inside his skull.

There was no long hallway, no flaming stage pots, no big screen TV or other Oz-type trappings. It was a nondescript office in an unmarked office building. Calley could tell the only purpose for the office was the sort of meeting that was about to take place. There were no computers and very little furniture. What furniture there was looked as if it were bought at Target or WalMart.

The curtain was a wrinkled piece of muslin, much the same as photographers use to drape portrait backgrounds. The light from a window was enough to cast a faint outline of "the boss" on the drape.

As they entered the room the boss said, "Please have a seat and introduce me to your associate."

"This is Calais Crowcroft. He's an old friend, and he now lives out there near Gibsonton. He knows a great deal about the place and what's happened so far, so we need not go into that. He knows a lot more about the operation. I filled him in on some, but not all, the details," said Pipare. "He definitely knows the implications of being here."

"Let me see if I understand your report," the boss said as they heard papers being shuffled.

"You've concluded that this-this-book, the focus of your investigation, is not the records of some Mafia meetings as believed by the deceased, but a book we've been looking for these past forty or fifty years? That's what you've concluded?"

"That's right," Barry responded.

He explained that the book wasn't available, but he'd seen photocopied pages from it. While it couldn't be conclusively proved to be what everyone was looking for, it seemed to him to be likely.

"If you'll look at Exhibit A in the report. Those are my notes from the photocopies. I—I didn't want to throw up any red flags so I didn't want to get a court order for the copies. After all, they're only copies and wouldn't make for very good evidence."

"That seems reasonable," the boss said. "Go ahead, tell me what these notes mean to you."

Pipare told him that although someone else might interpret them differently, he didn't see any other reasonable explanation. ATYGEN was a name for the Attorney General, Robert Kennedy and Bob was another reference to him.

"No one called him Bobby. That was a press invention. The nickname stuck from when he was a kid. Everyone called him Bob," explained Barry. "The quote is a famous JFK quote. The origin of it is a Jewish proverb. MoMo is Sam Giancana, Chairman of the Board is Frank Sinatra, the In-Law is Peter Lawford. Joe is probably Joseph Kennedy, SS is, no doubt the secret service, The Director is…uh, well, you know who that is…and…uh…the Pres—"

"You don't have to be a cryptographer to figure that one out," the boss said. "So you think this is the book we've been looking for all these years?"

"Damned if I know, but it certainly could be," declared Pipare. "There's more, one Ramón Villavicencio, later known as Ramón De Varo, a Cuban National, was in the right place at the right time to pick the book up. As nearly as I can find out, he was living as a homeless person in Hollywood at that time. Later he was discovered and became an unsuccessful movie actor, then went back to being a bum."

Barry told his boss that Ramón was related to the decedent and the book went to him when he died. Eventually the swaypole acrobat was involved in an accident that took his wife's life and he became unhinged.

"The word is that he hid the book in his trailer, and the book went out with him when he died. It was destroyed in the fire that Leon himself had set, and he took any knowledge of it with him by committing suicide," Barry explained.

"How did Villavicencio get the book?" asked the boss.

"No one knows, but it's my guess that he found it in a trash bin. As you know, the owner of the diary was hit in a pretty messy way and there was a hurried cleanup of the premises. I figure one of the perps tossed it as he was driving away."

"Yeah, it was a real mess, but through all of the talk and conspiracy theories, no one had caught on. That's the way these things typically go. You think there's a chance the diary is still out there somewhere?" said the boss.

"I'd say it's not much better than a ten per cent chance," said Barry. "My gut tells me if Leon had it to begin with, it was burned in the fire. At best, the photocopies are probably all that's left of it, assuming they're genuine to begin with."

"Even with odds like that, no one's going to be satisfied. There's our outfit, the CIA, the FBI, NSA, and a whole lot of other initial groups that would like to have it or be assured it went up in smoke. And don't forget the boys down in Texas, a bunch of Cubans, and a whole lot of politicians who would heave a sigh of relief if they knew for certain it's gone," said the boss.

"That must make it worth, I was going to say millions, but I'll bet billions wouldn't touch it," said Calley.

"I'm sure you could get a fairly decent government contract from one political party or another if you could turn that book over to them," said the boss with a mirthless chuckle. "Make Halliburton look like kindergarten players. The Director was able to get all of the tapes, at least we think he got all of them, together and burned them, so we dodged that bullet. You know Barry, The Director and maybe Hoffa had her place and about everywhere else she went wired. Talk about Watergate, those tapes could have really played hell with history. Now it's this damned book.

"It's the low-tech stuff that catches up every time," opined Calley.

"Not a word of this leaves this room. So far as everyone is concerned, this case is just an old nutty, depressed carny who hung himself. Case closed! And, Mr....ah...Crowcroft is it? I hope Mr. Pipare has made it clear to you what might happen if anyone were to leak this information or anything about this meeting."

"Oh, yes sir. Perfectly clear."

"Let me assure you that whatever happens to the leaker, it will be slow, painful and it will happen to his family and everyone around him, a scorched earth policy, if you know my meaning?"

As they were leaving, Calley turned to Barry. "Man, oh, man, holy shit fire—Marilyn Monroe's diary!"

"I didn't hear him say that's what it was," said Barry, positively.

"Oh, come on now, you know—"

"I didn't hear him say what the book was," said Barry with emphasized finality.

"You know, I wouldn't even want to touch it. There must be stuff in there that could cause a worldwide shit storm, stuff anyone would be curious about, but they really wouldn't want to know. Holy mondo-bizzaro, land of Oz."

"We know enough now to get us all killed. If we talked, there wouldn't be any investigation, charges filed, or a trial. Shit, they'd kill us, everyone we know and sow our fields with salt. I sure hope you don't talk in your sleep. So shut the hell up about it," cautioned Barry.

Lenya was in a blue funk for several days until Joey Judd

stopped by to say goodbye. The announcement caught everyone by surprise because there was never a hint that he would
ever leave Gibtown. He told them he was going back to Florida
to live with a nephew who was ill. He said his nephew had had
a stroke.

"John had his stroke a few months back, and he's not recov-
ering very quickly. He needs help getting around, and he needs
someone to do his shopping and to look after him. It'll give me
a chance to feel like I'm worth something," he announced. "It
just ain't the same around here with Leon gone anyway. Hell, I
can't even get a rise out of half the crowd around this dump."

"You'll lose your reputation if you start this late in life doing good works," chided Lenya. "I'll bet you're working some
kinda' spoof to worm your way into heaven."

"Hey, Joey Judd has 'asshole' written across his forehead.
When I get to the Pearlies, old Saint Peter's going to have one
of them 'if-you're-tall-enough-for-this' signs. If you're tall
enough for this, you can go on in. Don't matter what the game,
it's always gaffed against me and I always come up short." He
laughed more heartily than he should have.

"I know you can't bring yourself to say you'll miss me, so I
won't wait around for it."

Lenya broke down, puddled up, and took Joey into her arms.
"I'll miss ya Joey. I'll miss ya," she repeated with a sniffle,
and then held him at arm's length. "You wanta come back for
a visit, you can always stay with us. The rent'll only be a few
bucks. No one else who knows you will put up with your nasty
ass anyway." She began to sob in earnest, and then Joey started
to blubber.

"I gotta' get outa here," he said. My image is getting totally
ruined." He picked up a beat-up 1940s vintage suitcase and
headed out to a taxi that, unbeknownst to Lenya and Devey,

was waiting outside. As he got to the car, he turned, gave a military salute, and got into the passenger's seat.

"Wonder where he got the money to have a taxi come all the way out here," said Devey.

Chapter 39

Barry dropped Calley off at Lenya's place and drove on to Charleston. Calley arrived just in time for supper but he told Lenya he was tired and wasn't hungry. They had just fixed enough for two, but Lenya insisted that Calley was actually hungry. He felt sort of guilty for eating, but the food was great.

After the meal, Lenya went to the deck and took up her position in the recliner to read a magazine. Devey and Calley sat on the bench with their backs to her, watching the red disk of an exhausted sun slipping into the foothills on the horizon.

"You know, Joey Judd left today. Dropped by to say goodbye. Kind of sudden, I guess. All too sudden," Lenya said.

"I suppose after Leon's death he needed a change of scenery," offered Calley.

"Going down to Florida to take care of a relative who had a stroke down there. He's gonna' help him get around and be sort of a companion, I guess."

"Can't imagine a pit bull for a companion," mused Calley. "Nice evening anyway."

"Don't nice evening me. What happened? Where did you two go?" began Devey.

Calley looked at her and, with a smile, told her, "If I tell you, I'd have to kill you."

"That gives me a big pain in the ass every time someone says it. It's a hell of a thing to say. Now, don't give me any of that secret agent bullshit either, I've had it up to here with that shit. It had to do with Leon, didn't it?

Calley hoped the pause would be taken as a 'no'. It wasn't.

"Didn't it?" she insisted.

"Yes, and I can't talk about it."

"They swore you to secrecy?" Devey persisted.

"Something like that, but I can't talk about it, that's all," he said.

"Can't or won't?" Devey left in a snit.

Later that evening, after hours of prying, Calley decided to tell her something just to get her off his back. He knew she'd never let him rest until she learned at least a bit about what was going on. Hopefully feeding her little tidbits would satisfy her and allow him back into her good graces.

"Look, this is so secret. If any breath of this gets out all of us will be in danger, understand?"

"Yeah, I—"

"UNDERSTAND?" Calley snapped impatiently, more loudly than he realized. Lenya stirred from her magazine and looked their way, but went back to reading.

"There's no need to scream at me," Devey whispered.

"Yes, there is. You just don't know, you have no idea how serious all of this is. I'm telling you this, but you have to know if it gets out, it could endanger all of us.

"Leon had this book. We're sure it was burned up in the fire, but it seems to be a big deal with some of the higher ups. Remember how Leon was always talking that paranoid stuff about the CIA, FBI and Mafia? It looks now like it wasn't paranoia after all. The secret agent types might have been after something Leon had. That's what we think they were after," he explained.

"Oh, really," Devey said in a tone that suggested she was being had. She didn't believe a word of it.

"Really," Calley said, hoping to put the matter to rest.

Of course it only piqued her interest.

"So Mr. Hot Shit, what if I told you I don't know what it is but I think I know where it is?"

"I'd say you were lying to me, just to get my goat so I'll reveal something. I know you don't know shit about it. You didn't know about it until I just told you. I'm not that stupid. Anyway it burned up in the fire if it ever was to begin with and I seriously doubt if it really amounted to anything," Calley said with conviction.

"I know where it is," Devey returned in a sing-song childish voice.

"Look, miss smarty drawers, this is serious shit. You need to know there are people out there who would kill you—kill all of us in a heartbeat if they even thought you knew anything about this, let alone where it is."

"You really aren't kidding are you?" she said guiltily.

"If you know something, you should tell me. If you don't, you should clam up and keep it to yourself. Don't kid around with this shit," cautioned Calley.

"Well, I…ah…I don't know exactly what it is, or even where it may be. Let's just say I know who does, or at least who should know. Now you've really got me scared, really, really frightened."

Calley told her she should be scared and to get serious now and tell him what she knew. "Who do you think has it?"

Devey glanced over her shoulder to the dozing Lenya and

cautiously motioned with her thumb and nodded in Lenya's direction. She told Calley that Lenya had told her that Leon had given her a bag of stuff for safekeeping a long time ago. And she really didn't know what was in the bag. She didn't think either of them knew for sure.

"It makes sense, though," Devey said in her defense. "What else would Leon have wanted her to keep for him? What else would he be so desperate to get out of his trailer? Did you ever see inside that rat's nest? He sure wasn't interested in clearing out junk."

So, Calley thought, Lenya, one of the main munchkins, might just be sitting on a time bomb.

He looked around at the peacefully napping little person. It made his heart sink to know they might be in grave danger, and the whole thing could go off at any time with all of them in the blast zone. Not too many days ago he was happily traveling toward Dillweed without a care in the world, fat, dumb, and happy. Now he was embroiled in what had the potential for becoming a nightmare of global proportions. If the diary contained what they thought, even a paragraph could bring down a government, give insights into the Kennedy assassinations, and involve vast right and left wing conspiracies, explain our involvement in Viet Nam, disrupt treaties, and involve the Mafia. It could sink the Cuban government, implicate the former Soviet Union, and point fingers at our own government, the President. The possibilities were endless.

Chapter 40

That evening around the kitchen table, Lenya asked what Calley and Devey were discussing out there on the deck.

"You got a little loud at one point there, I though maybe you two were going to take over squabbling duties since Leon took the big dirt nap. I don't know what Joey will do with himself now that Leon is gone. Leon was the only one crazy enough to put up with that little bastard."

"Oh, it was nothing. Devey wanted to know what Barry Pipare and I had been up to all day. I went to his office with him and she wanted to know what we were doing. There's so much of the stuff that he does that's secret, it doesn't leave much for me to talk about," said Calley.

"He told me one thing you should know about though—" began Devey.

"Maybe she doesn't need to know," Calley interrupted, giving her an angry look.

Devey shot him a look that could have burned paint off the wall.

"I think you should tell her the basics anyway. She has a right to know. She's the one in most danger."

174

"Hey, hey, let's not blow this out of all proportion. It's dangerous, but, well, I suppose you're right, but the less you guys know about this, the better off you are. You really don't understand and I don't know all that much myself."

Calley went on to tell her about "a missing item." He didn't tell her what he thought the item might be or its importance. She already suspected something was up, but there wasn't much point in telling her the whole story and exposing her anymore than he already had.

"Devey says Leon gave you a bag to keep for him. We're thinking a book might be in it. Do you know anything about it?"

"I got the bag," said Lenya. "It's big enough to hold a book, but I never looked inside. I always figured Leon would want it back, and I'd be better off if I could say to him, or anyone else, I didn't know what was in it. I'd have done the same if anyone gave me anything for safekeeping."

Calley began to caution her, "If you want to look in the bag, there's nothing to stop you. I suppose with Leon gone, no one knows or cares what's in there. I suppose the bag and its contents are yours to do with as you like. All that said, I still say, you're better off not knowing anything about the contents of that bag."

"Is this…this item worth anything?" asked Lenya.

"More than you'll ever know, more than your wildest dreams. But I think you'd be far better off to burn the bag and die a pauper rather than risk trying to sell it."

"Well, if I were to keep it, I could sell it, couldn't I? There's nothing illegal about selling what you've inherited is there? You see, I know this guy—he buys and sells old stuff on eBay. He'd be able to tell us what we might get out of it. Maybe we could even sell it on eBay. I'd be more than willing to share—"

"Lenya," Calley said firmly and gently, "this isn't the kind of thing you'd sell on eBay. Its value isn't that it's an antique, or collector's item, although I'm sure some collectors would be interested. This is the kind of thing that political Machiavellian-types would die for. It's the stock and trade of secret societies, terrorists, thugs and other world leaders. It could contain infinite power and an infinite potential for evil. My best advice is to burn it before its inherent evil finds a new owner."

"Hey, now you've got me hot and wet. This kind of shit really rings my chimes and gets me cranking. I'm not about to burn something that might let us all retire in luxury. Hell, we'll buy out Gibtown and move every down and out, out of work, carny in. We'll have cars, planes, take a vacation every—"

"Just listen to yourself," interrupted Devey. "A few minutes ago, you were living a peaceful existence in a rural community without a care in the world. Now you want to chuck it all for another spin at the wheel, another chance for fame. What would you do, start your own show with your own Ten-in-One? Would you be the headliner, the star? Princess of the Pygmies?

"I'm sorry; I'm so terribly sorry, Lenya. I didn't mean that. I got carried away. It sounded awful, but what you're saying doesn't sound much better."

"Don't be sorry. I've heard worse. You two think you have a handle on the world, don't you? You've never seen it from down here. You've never had to put up with the stares or seen the look on people's faces and heard their shitty comments. Maybe you never had to live from hand to mouth not knowing if you'd make it to the next town or the next meal.

"Now I've got a chance to be...to be, I don't know, bigger. It's a chance for people to look up to me for a change. I know it sounds awful, but to be somebody, at least for a little while."

Calley said, "Do what you want to do, Lenya. Just be careful. Don't tell this to just anyone. Go ahead carefully. Test the water to see what it might bring. Move slowly and deliberately, and leave yourself plenty of room to back out if it starts going down badly."

"After all the preaching you did about secrecy, about the danger and how we all might be killed over this damned thing, I can't believe you just told her that," complained Devey.

Calley motioned palms down, pushing his hands lower. "Later, Devey, we'll talk later."

Later Calley would tell her it was the only way, short of stealing the book from her and perhaps killing her. She was determined, and the best they could look forward to now was to play along and hope for the best.

"Go ahead, get in touch with the guy you know. Don't tell him what you have. You really don't know what you have, for sure," Calley said.

"That's right, and whatever is in that bag is going to stay in there until I find out some more about what it really is and what it's worth. Now, so I don't have to go digging it out, you tell me what it is. What's all the mystery and dark forces you're talking about? Is this some sort of Devil worship, spell casting, demonology thing? A tome of medieval end-of-times predictions? What is it you think I have?"

"In a way, it might be all of those things," Calley said. What you may have in that old bag you have stowed away somewhere—and I don't want to know where—could be Marilyn Monroe's diary."

"Bullshit. I thought you said it's earth shattering; valuable, something powerful people will kill for. A dead actress's account of the times she missed her period? I can see a collector might pay a few hundred thousand for it, but I don't think anyone's going to kill someone to get their hands on it," she said, laughing.

Calley just shook his head at her naïve lack of understanding. He explained that Marilyn was traveling in some pretty fast company near the end of her life. She was involved with everything from Mafia Dons to Presidents and would-be Presidents. She wasn't the bimbo blonde she pretended to be for public consumption, but a world-wise politically savvy woman. She was a woman who was dallying with socialists, world-class philanderers and political movers and shakers, a paramour to a president and a president to be. And, if the rumors had any substance, a number of people who would rather she were a corpse than a talking blonde bombshell.

"Lenya, she was sleeping with at least two of the most powerful men in the world, playing one off the other. That's not some dumb slut we're talking about. She had connections through them and Hollywood that ran through several Mafia families and a number of foreign governments. Now, do you get it?"

"Yeah, I get it, but that was a long time ago. It's over, forgotten, kaput, as my daddy used to say."

"Yeah," said Calley, "kaput."

Chapter 41

Eitan Abramawitz's family came to America in the late 30s for the same reason many European Jews left their homeland. People like Lenya Klebb's father were putting the handwriting on the walls. Krystalnacht was the capstone of a long string of injustices that made the decision easy. The young Eitan was fortunate enough to read about what happened in Europe from afar. Names like Babi Yar, Auschwitz-Birkenau and Treblinka were, for him, unknown places on a map and what was happening to his extended family was equally unknown, until much later.

However, once again goose-stepping troops and the smell of *einsatzgruppen* was wafting through the 21st century Middle East. Eitan hid among his books and thought of the slogan of the Jewish Defense League, "Never Again," but here it was, beginning again. It seemed as if all it took was one man to start it, but any one man was powerless to stop it.

The man who Lenya Klebb knew was Eitan Abramawitz. She met him when she was a child and she went to his bookshop at every chance to browse and to skim. She went to read and take shelter from her brutal father. She went until he found out, and she never went again until she was much older. She never understood why her father had such hatred for him. It was beyond a child's understanding, beyond the understanding of any human heart, but not beyond her father's.

When Calley Crowcroft mentioned the book, she immediately thought of the old man who made sure she had books to read when she was a child. When her thoughts turned to Mr. Abramawitz, she could immediately smell the musty perfume of the old shop's books and the garlic on the old man's breath.

She thought long and hard about involving him in what Calley cautioned as being extremely dangerous. How could an old book be so dangerous? How could the dead words of a long-dead actress portend death and destruction on an apocalyptic scale? Surely Calley had exaggerated, trying to scare her, or perhaps he was being overly cautious. Surely no harm could come from merely asking.

Calley freaked out at the women's naiveté when Devey told him Lenya was going to call an old friend in Miami to discuss the matter.

"Don't you two get it? You still don't have a clue, do you? Look, the phone in this place is bugged. That's right, everything, anything that goes out and comes in, is recorded. If you want to get hired assassins in here after our asses, the quickest way I know to go about it is to get on that phone and start blabbing."

"I suppose she could use a pay phone. We'll drive several miles down the road and find one. That place where Gid stopped for gas had one out front. We could use that, couldn't we?" Devey asked.

"I suppose so. I don't think they would tap a pay phone and surely not one that far away. If you two are determined to get us all in hot water, go ahead. Take her down there and place

the call. Don't be forever on the phone, though. And Devey—
for future reference—

"Yeah, I know, you told me so."

From the end of a telephone line and at least one culture
away came the voice of an ancient "Abramawitz and Son."

"Who is this?" asked Lenya.

"Eitan Abramawitz, you got Abramawitz's book store."

"Mr. Abramawitz, this is Lenya—Lenya Klebb. You remember?"

"Don't know any Klebb."

"Little Lenya, years ago I—"

"Little Lenya." A light went on, and she could feel his smile
through the miles of telephone connections.

"You remember!"

"Of course I remember liebling. Who could forget the Nazi's
daughter? Oh, I'm sorry, I didn't mean—"

"Yes you did. You meant it because that's exactly what he
was. No use lying about him now that he's gone. He was a real
arschloch putz." She could feel his warm smile again.

"Well, well, how are you doing? It's so good to hear the
voice of someone from the old days," he gushed with a hint
of Yiddish accent that had lost its edge in the years of dealing
with the American public.

"Abramawitz and Son. I'm impressed. I didn't know you
had a son," said Lenya.

"Don't be. Don't have one. It just makes me sound more
important when I answer the phone like that. Is there something I can do for you, Lennie? You know you were always my
favorite kid. A daughter like you, I never had. You would have
made me proud."

"Mr. Abramawitz, I have a book—I think I have a book. I

would like for you to help me decide what it's worth. I don't have it in front of me, but maybe if I give you a description—"

"Eitan. It's Eitan. I'm old enough already; Mr. Abramawitz sounds even older. I don't know how much I could tell you long-distance. Can you send it to me? You could insure it, so if it's lost—"

"No, no, I don't have it. I just want some ideas, that's all. I know you'd have to see it to tell me more. This is just to get me started."

"What do you have, my dear? What's the date?"

"It's not a regular book, more like a collector's item. It's the diary of a famous movie star. It dates somewhere in the early 60s I'd say. I can't say who the movie star is now, but she was popular in the 50s and 60s," Lenya told him.

"Lennie, you don't give me much to go on," he said, "If it's a Grace Kelly, that could be worth a fortune, particularly if it has some tasty tidbits in it. You know, gossip about the prince or Gary Cooper, Clark Gable, Bill Holden, David Niven, Ray Milland—whoever. I think they all got a little piece of the virgin princess at one time or another. It would be a scandal then, not so much now. Historical interest though.

If it's a Lauren Bacall, not so much. Even an Audrey Hepburn won't bring that kind of money. If it's a Marilyn Monroe you could strike it rich. If you got one of hers, it could be a goldmine, two or three goldmines even. The rest of that era is pretty boring to most people. Remember, as far as the public is concerned, it's ancient history. A Kelly or Monroe is what you should be hoping for."

"Well, Eitan, that's a start," she assured him.

"Not much of a start. If you have a goody, be sure and let me know. I know buyers if you want to sell."

"If it's a Kelley what might it be worth?"

"Like I said, it would depend on content and how juicy it is. I'd say in the hundreds of thousands," Eitan said.

"And if it's a Monroe?"

There was a long pause.

"Lennie, we're old friends, you and me. If you have a Monroe diary from the time of her death, don't let anyone know you have it. Put it somewhere where it's safe and call me. Better yet, come and see me."

"What would it be worth?"

"*Es ken zany*—time will tell—but there are lots of people who'd be interested. Putting it on the market would be like selling the Hope Diamond. Very valuable, but not sell-able, and sure to attract a whole lot of attention of the wrong kind. In this case, you wouldn't want the attention it might attract, if you get my meaning."

"Eitan, please don't say or do anything until I call you again."

By some unknown means, the word passes through a backlot faster than over the Internet. It's as if there's a global psychic connection somewhere that binds showfolk together. Of course, many of them know someone who knows someone who's related to someone else, but it's uncanny nonetheless.

In less than a week after it happed, Lenya learned of Joey's accident. He'd been killed riding, of all things, a bicycle. It was a small one used by a neighbor kid that Joey was riding on a lark. No one saw it happen, but the police reported that he was riding under an overhanging support on a jungle gym and forgot to duck. He was struck in the left temple and never regained consciousness.

Too tall to get under a gym bar, thought Lenya. Ain't that some real shit. Too short for this life but just tall enough to die.

She wondered if he made it through the Pearly Gates. Maybe there is a special back gate for short little pricks.

Of course, Lenya and Calley didn't believe the story for a minute. The sudden deaths of Leon and Joey were all too convenient. Convenient because they were both connected to Gibtown, and they both knew something about what was under Lenya's trailer.

Under Lenya's doublewide there was a foundation of cast resin stone. Not the cheap vacuum formed stuff you see at the Home Depot or Lowes, but durable fiberglass reinforced resin. Near the back door, close to the water heater was a hidden access panel. The purpose of the panel was to provide access to the trailer's water supply and water heater. An extra layer of fiberglass insulation was placed over and around the valves in case of freezing. Over the top of the fiberglass was another layer, and sandwiched between them was an overnight bag not much bigger than a Dopp Kit.

Inside the bag was a folded shopping bag and inside that was a small, bound book. Over the top of the overnight bag was a cheap .22 caliber revolver that Lenya's husband had given her. She knew he had stolen it, and she had hidden it away and, almost as an afterthought, she hid the bag at the same time.

If Ramón had been able to read longhand, he would have seen the blurred name inside the book. He might have read Norma Jean scrawled under it.

Lenya had never seen the contents of either bag, and she had left it there since the time a depressed, agitated, and paranoid Leon Riluttante had given it to her, and there it had stayed. She hadn't gone near it for fear it was filled with illicit drugs.

Chapter 42

Men in Black are no strangers to The Mountain State. The
MIB supposedly intimidated a reporter in West Virginia to stop
writing articles in newspapers about the MIB's presence in
Pinewood, and MIB were seen both before and after the col-
lapse of the Silver Bridge in Point Pleasant.

Barry Pipare, with his dark, cheap investigator's suit and
darker shades, was the picture of a Man In Black. Ironically,
he didn't qualify as a true West Virginia MIB because he
was—black. Days passed, and Lenya fidgeted. She was afraid
to do anything and afraid not to. She was sure she'd seen men
driving by in dark cars, men in black suits, wearing black sun-
glasses behind tinted windows.

One of them she already knew. Barry Pipare came back to
ask questions. He quizzed her about Leon and his relationship
with Joey. He made references to an undiscovered package that
he knew Leon had hidden somewhere.

Lenya was sure Pipare somehow knew about her call to
Eitan. Was it paranoia, or should she just assume every phone
was tapped? She knew she was starting to think like Leon and
she was beginning to understand Leon better with every pass-

ing day. Living near Gibtown and its dark mysteries only lent to her suspicions of being listened to and watched. She was sure of it as she felt herself spinning into the grip of paranoia. All sorts of conspiracy theories developed as she tried to put each one out of mind.

She was convinced Joey Judd had implicated her somehow and told Pipare that he was sure she had the original book. Now it was, to her a certainty, she knew Pipare had her under surveillance. Men in Black were watching at every turn they were everywhere. This wasn't such a radical notion so far as Gibtown was concerned. She had the uneasy feeling that they might even be able to read her thoughts.

Lenya wanted to go to the hidden panel in her trailer under-pinning and drag out the miserable bag and examine its con-tents, but the thought of seeing it and learning for certain of the contents made her ill. She feared she would become like Leon, lose her mind entirely and slip into the abyss of depression. If she'd been alone that might have happened but Devey and Calley had kept her centered. They buoyed her up with their unconditional friendship. She had worked herself into such a state that Devey and Calley decided something had to be done.

"Devey has money that her aunt and father left. Why don't you call your book dealer friend and have him come for a visit and take a look at the thing? I know you're afraid to leave here and go to him. We'll be more than glad to pay for an airline ticket and drive to Charleston or Clarksburg to get him."

Lenya protested at first and said it would be like taking charity, but eventually gave in to Devey's convincing argu-ments. Lenya finally agreed to call Abramawitz and invite him to examine the book. She would offer him an appraisal fee for looking it over and a fat commission on the sale if he would undertake locating a buyer.

It was after lunch when Devey, Calley, and Lenya traveled to the remote gas station. There, surrounded by Devey and Calley, Lenya picked up the phone and stared at the dialing buttons. Reluctantly she dialed Eitan's number. The phone rang several times until finally someone picked up on the other end.

"Abramawitz and Son," said a female voice.

"May I speak to Eitan Abramawitz?" Lenya said.

"I'm afraid that's not possible. To whom am I speaking please?"

"I'm Lenya Klebb, an old friend of his. Would you please put him on?"

"I'm sorry Lenya," she said gently, Mr. Abramawitz passed away."

Shocked by the news, Lenya said, "It must have been quite sudden. Heart attack, stroke? How did he die?"

"The doctor said it was a brain hemorrhage. You're quite correct; it was very sudden. None of us knew he had any living family, but a niece called from Austria and settled his affairs, paid his debts and other expenses, and paid to have him cremated. It was all completed within a matter of a couple of days."

"What?" asked Lenya. "Did I hear you correctly? Cremated?"

"Cremated. It all happed so fast. There was no time to get very much done. He was here working one day and gone the next. The attorneys just hired me to answer the phone until the business is closed."

Lenya hung up the phone and wiped a tear from her eye with the heel of her hand. Neither Calley nor Devey had ever seen her this way. A mask of anger clouded her face, and her eyes focused somewhere far away.

"Brain hemorrhage my ass," she muttered with a hiss.

"You don't think that's what killed him?" said Devey.

"Eitan was as Orthodox as they come. He would never have permitted anyone to send him off in any way similar to what the Nazis had done," she said with an animal-like snarl. "Call that Pipare guy—that, secret agent friend of yours Calley. Tell him to get his ass out here. I want to talk to him, one-on-one."

Chapter 43

Lenya decided to meet Pipare by herself. She would tell
Devey and Calley anything she felt they needed to know later.

"First of all, let's not start with the traditional CIA-FBI or
whatever it is crap, alright? Let's assume I wasn't born yes-
terday and, although I may be small, my brain isn't," Lenya
began. "So let's not get off into the what-you-can't-tell-me
world, okay?"

"Hey, lady, you're the one who wanted to meet. Ask what
you want. Say what you got on your mind. You won't know
what I don't want to tell you anyway. I don't mean any disrespect, but that's just the way the world is," said Pipare.

"I think we see eye to eye. First question, is my phone
tapped?"

Pipare said with a snort, "of course it is, your phone and every other phone in a thirty-mile radius—tapped, recorded 24/7.
Anything else?"

"Yeah, who does the tapping?"

"We—the state investigators, the FBI, CIA, NSA, ATF and
I expect the Mafia, KGB, DGI, Islamic Terrorists, Hamas,
Mossad, forces who are pro-Cuban, and a whole raft of other

foreign interests maybe. Sorry, Lenya, but that's the way it is in Gibtown. You chose to live in a centriole of surveillance. Everyone wants to know everything about the folks who live here. You people who are on the fringes of the town proper are caught up in it by proximity, not so much because of any direct interest," Pipare explained.

"Guilt by association, huh?"

"Not really. You just happen to be where you are, that's all. It's where the action—no, the center of interest is."

"Did you have anything to do with the death of Leon Riluttante? I don't mean, did you kill him; I mean, did you have anything to do with it?"

"No."

"Do you know who did?"

"I have an idea or two, but I don't have any direct knowledge of who did it or why, just suspicions at this point."

Barry explained they were convinced persons outside the law, perhaps organized crime, either Russian, American, or even Mexicans or Cubans, made a hit on Leon. There's little chance it was terrorists or any group aligned with Middle Eastern terrorism, but it was always a possibility. He and some of his colleagues are convinced the best guess is American Mafia, and the reason for the hit was he either had some information or knew where to find it.

"Do you intend to investigate Leon's death?" asked Lenya.

"Nope, and no one else I know of will either."

"I suppose Leon is too little of a fish to worry about, huh?"

"Look, Lenya, let me explain it to you this way. There are a lot of folks out there, including those I work for, who are relieved Leon is out of the picture. Moreover, they'd be more than pleased if Leon's trailer fire burned up whatever Leon had."

"So that's it? Little fish dies, his stuff goes up in flames and everybody gets away clean, fat, dumb, and happy? All tied up neat and tidy," said Lenya.

"Everybody was fairly pleased until the time you got on the phone to Eitan Abramawitz. Now all of those dark characters, and some lighter ones, are back in the hunt. I'd say some of them are convinced what Leon had is still around, and I'd bet there's a goodly percentage of them who think you know where it is."

"Well, I don't know where it is, and for all I know, it doesn't even exist," Lenya said positively.

"M.B.E." Barry exclaimed.

"What?"

"Male bovine excrement," he replied. "So, let's see, you called Eitan to discuss the weather in Florida. Now who's trying to bullshit who? Come on, Lenya, you might not know where it is exactly, or what it is exactly, but Leon told you enough to get your imagination going. And that might be just enough to get all those forces out there after your little bitty ass."

"So, you or someone you work for capped Eitan? Is that about it?"

Pipare smiled. "I'm not going to grace a question like that with an answer."

"So what am I supposed to do?"

"Lay low. Don't go near the book if you have it. Watch your back, stay among friends, arm yourself, and wait. Don't try to run, that's going to draw more attention. Besides, there's no place to run to. That's about the best you can do. Hell, it's all you can do. Stay safe."

Johnny Stampanato and Louis Del Vecchio were relaxing

in Tampa, Florida. Miami was hot, too hot for Johnny and Louis, and it wasn't the weather. Tampa wasn't paradise but it wasn't Gibtown, Florida either. It had a whole different set of sideshow freaks. Emilio Porrello had warned them they were to stay away from any resorts or gambling casinos while they were in Florida, and that had put a serious crimp in their activities.

"Hell, we might as well be in Webster," complained Louis.

"They got a hell of a flea market there. You into flea markets?" asked Johnny.

"I mean this freakin' place is getting' on my nerves. I need to get back to the city, back to Jersey, someplace where people know me."

"Give it a few days. There ain't no heat gonna' rise off killin' that little guy on a bicycle. Give it a few days, and we'll go back north," Johnny assured him.

"One thing gets me about these jobs. Ya never know why the guy's gettin' whacked. An old geezer who liked books and who tha' hell would want a little fella' who likes riding bicycles whacked? Don't make no sense ta' me."

"Well, get your ass ready, because as soon as we get back, the boss has got another one for us. Seems like a lot of action all of a sudden. That's the trouble with this business. It's either feast or famine," complained Johnny.

"I ain't complainin', mind you. Don't get me wrong; I'd rather be working than sittin' aroun' some fleabag motel all day. I'd like to get out to da' dog track or go to that Hard Rock place. What ya' say?"

"Ain't nothing but trouble if you go there. We ain't even supposed to be in Florida. We get spotted it's gonna be our asses. The boss has guys here who are lookin' out for him and are looking for work. I don't want to have to deal with any of them. You wind up out there in the bay with crabs eatin' your eyeballs out like they wuz grapes," Johnny said.

"You're right, like always, Johnny, you're right. I'm goin' down to the pool and look over some wet bikinis."

Chapter 44

Days passed and finally a call from New York came. The two hit men were to meet with the boss at the usual place, and he would tell them what they had to do next. The flight was always like magic for Louis, whose dad drove down I-95 when he took the family to Orlando or Daytona for Easter. The trip usually took a couple of days, and they would stay overnight somewhere in North Carolina.

Johnny and Louis took up their familiar positions in the Art Deco waiting room of Emilio Porrello and Louis took up his favorite pastime of trading insults with Zvonimira Draganja. Louis was having a great time, but Zvon wasn't amused.

"Kinda' name is Draganja? Sounds like something you'd call a guy who dresses up in women's clothes."

"That's a drag queen, she said dryly. Weren't you in a movie once? No, that must have been Devine. You look something like her. You know, I could swear I saw you dressed up in that movie *Trash*. Yeah, I think Joe Dallesandro was doing it to you in that one."

Confused, and definitely not an avant garde film buff, Louis decided he was in over his head and broke off the conversation. Meanwhile, Johnny was off in a corner trying to hide behind a copy of *GQ* when a buzzer on Zvonmira desk sounded.

"You may show the gentlemen in, Miss Draganja," said the boss.

"Don't see no gentlemen here," said Louis.

"Wasn't funny the last time," said Zvonmira, "and it's even less funny now. Get your dead butt in there before the boss chews it off."

"Have a seat, boys. You guys have been doing me proud. Super job, just great. I'm gonna' see to it that you get a bonus when this next job is done—if you don't screw it up."

"I—" began Johnny.

"Did I ask you a question?"

"Uh...no,"

"That's right. When I want to hear from either one of you, I'll let you know. Don't open your big yaps until I say. You got that?"

"Hey, Loo-ee, you big dumb shit!" the boss shouted. "You got that?"

"Yes, sir, I got it, I got it."

"This one isn't quite as simple at the last ones. It isn't a set-up, so to speak. You're the only ones in on it and, if you get caught, you're on your own. No one is going to be there to guide you in or bail you out. You mess this one up and we all swing. You mess this one up and, before I go, I'll make sure you two suffer before you die," he said with a grim smile.

Both men had heard stories about how Porrello loved to use an electric drill, even when no information was to be gained. He just enjoyed it.

Porrello began to lay out the next job. He explained this one was different because there were three people living in the home and he preferred only the person to be hit would be taken out.

"You might have to take all of them down, but that would be awfully messy. You catch my drift?" he continued without waiting for a response from his slower colleagues. "Messy is what none of us need; messy draws too much heat. It's an option, though, if things get complicated and they get involved and have to be shut up, it's a last resort."

Louis raised a hand like a kid in the second grade and awaited recognition.

"Louis?"

"What if we've gotta' wack 'em all?"

"Don't even think about it. Like I said, last resort. The person to be terminated is one Lenya Leota Klebb. You're gonna' love this one, Louis. She's a midget."

"I got no problem with that."

"That's not what my sources tell me," the boss interrupted. "This isn't from your buddy here, you understand, but it got back to me that you felt sorry for the little guy on the bicycle."

"I guess it was just that I felt bad about takin' that big pipe and wackin' him. It was like I was hittin' a little kid. Besides, you don't call 'em midgets anyways. That's not nice. It's little people. They like that a lot better," Louis Del Vecchio fearlessly admonished the boss.

"I'll try and remember that the next time we have to wack one of them," Porrello said with his grim smile.

He continued by telling them the house would be near the site of their last effort, near what was left of Leon Riluttante's trailer. Their mark would be tough to separate from a couple who moved in as companions. He explained they were younger and perhaps tougher targets than Lenya Klebb. Porrello suggested they kidnap her when the couple wasn't around.

Perhaps they could get the job done while the couple was away shopping. They would take her somewhere remote and try to get her to reveal where the stuff was that Leon Riluttante had given her to hide.

"You might pick up one of them cordless drills. They convince a person to talk real fast when they hear it whining near their head. I don't figure you'll be able to get a straight answer out of her, but even if you do, or if you don't, it won't matter if she's out of the picture. Johnny can use his icepick or you can use your Ruger to complete the job.

"Just a neat little hole, you understand. No messy shotguns or high-powered stuff. You're gonna bury her out there someplace, so I'm not concerned how she's killed. Just make sure she isn't found. This isn't brain surgery," he chuckled, picturing the drill and the irony. "There's lots of empty strip mines and abandoned wells out there. Case the area for a few days and pick a nice lonely spot.

"Any questions?"

There was a long pause while Louis and Johnny looked at each other and shrugged.

"If not, gentlemen, this meeting is concluded," said Porrello. "And Johnny, ditch that big black Mercedes. Makes you guys look like a couple of hoods. Get a Taurus."

Chapter 45

"Lenya, when we first got here, you mentioned you had a shotgun," said Calley.

"I did? I don't remember—"

"You said you sent a potential home invader on his way with a 12-gauge load of rock salt."

"Oh, that. That was just bullshit. I just wanted to scare you a little. Let you know what a bad ass I am."

"So you don't have a shotgun?"

"Oh, I got a shotgun, all right. And that ain't all. I got a 9mm Glock to boot."

"Holy shit, Lenya, do you know how to use them? Have you ever had to use them?"

"Damn right. An expert, the Mister, taught me. He showed me how to load them and shoot 'em and clean 'em, too. I never shot anyone, you understand, just targets and tin cans. But I can shoot real good."

"Where are they now?" Calley asked.

"I'm not getting them out, but they're in my bedroom. Loaded, shells in the chambers. Like I always say, I don't mind gettin' laid if I get paid, but ain't no man alive who's gonna rape me. And I'll put up with someone stealing some little stuff, but I got my limit. Ain't nobody hurtin' this little lady."

"Okay, okay, Lenya," Calley said soothingly. "I was just seeing if you had a way to protect yourself. I should have known not to worry."

"Anyone comes after me, they'll get a double-barrel load of double-ought in their face or a 9 mm hole in the head. I don't take prisoners and leave people for the police to question. I know a guy who learned that one the hard way.

"I knew a ride jockey once who shot some gilly who come poking around his place. He thought he'd be kind and shot him in the foot. The ride jock got a year in the slammer and is still paying that son-of-a-bitch's way."

"We just don't want to go off and leave you here—" began Devey.

"I'm not worried about Lenya," said Calley, "but I'm beginning to worry about anyone who would try something."

No one noticed a blue Taurus traveling through the region. Tourists used them, and they were a common rental. The only noticeable difference was the dark tinted windows Louis insisted on.

Johnny and Louis stayed in Charleston and traveled to the Gibtown area so they would arrive in late afternoon. They were aware of Lenya's doublewide and did a fast drive-by to check on entrances, but never returned. They spent most of their time trying to look like tourist hikers who were exploring the countryside while they were on the lookout for a good out-of-the-way burial place. There was no scarcity of such places near Gibtown.

They finally chose an abandoned gas well. There was a small pond that had been used for drainage and drilling mud, and they figured the earthen dam would make a dandy place for a shallow grave. The soil had already been disturbed, so a fresh grave wouldn't stand out. Some large rocks nearby could be piled on to assure animals didn't get to the remains. The place was close to a road, so if they had to carry the body, it wouldn't have to be carried all that far. Louis told Johnny that he intended to make her walk to the pond, and he'd use his .22 to finish the job right where they would bury her.

"We could dig the grave beforehand and save some time," he suggested.

"Nope, I ain't digging no grave for some kid or game warden to stumble onto," said Johnny. "You know what Mr. Porrello said about messy?"

With the matter settled about where to dispose of the body, the pair headed for Gibsonton. There they toured the town and stopped at the market to schmooze with the clerk. After a long conversation, beginning with the quality of the weather and ending with the county's hunting and fishing possibilities. He asked about Lenya.

"I've know Lenya for quite some time," he told the clerk. "We go back to the old carny days. Hear she's got a couple living in with her now."

By this time, the clerk was persuaded that the slick-talking Johnny was the person he presented himself to be, an affable, friendly talker.

"Yep," he said, "they come over here for groceries every Thursday, do her shopping, just like clockwork. That'd never do for my wife. She goes to the store about every other day, sometimes a couple of times a day. Says she forgets stuff. Not that pair, though. They got a list, and they stick to it. For them it's just like clockwork."

Louis, who had been hanging out in the back of the store,

joined Johnny as they prepared to leave.

"Nice meeting you," said Johnny.

"You going to pay for that?" said the clerk.

"What?" asked a surprised Louis.

"The bottle of pop you drank and the magazine you were reading."

"He forgets what day it is. Here, I'll pay for it," Johnny offered.

"I didn't take his freakin' magazine," Louis protested.

"This ain't no lieberry" began the clerk.

Johnny could see Louis doing a slow burn and he seemed to be reaching for his .22.

Shooting Louis a look that could kill, Johnny interrupted again saying, loudly, "I'll pay for it. I said I'll pay for it. Now shut up." He added special emphasis on the shut up.

Outside, Johnny grabbed Louis and pinched him in the soft under portion of his upper arm. "You dumb ass, you trying to attract attention? Everything was going smooth as silk. Now you gave him a reason to remember you. You're the big ugly ass shmuck who called attention to himself.

"Ow, Johnny, that hurts! Geez, I'm sorry, Johnny. I didn't mean—"

Johnny gave him a slap to the back of the head. "You're gonna get us killed one of these days. Now straighten up!"

Johnny Stampanato was achieving a degree of fame as "The Iceman" because Louis had been talking to his friends too much. Louis "The Lout" Del Vecchio would probably always be "The Lout" because his image was almost as retarded as he was.

The two traveled to Gibtown in anticipation of Calley and Devey's shopping trip on Thursday. Their intention was to practice a dry run so they could establish a timeline. Arriving early in the morning, they were lurking in a line of trees where they could see Lenya's home.

"There they go," said Louis. "They ain't even takin' the car, they're pushing a shopping cart. They're gonna' walk all that way over to town. That's gonna' take a while," he said pushing the stem on an old-fashioned stopwatch.

Exactly two hours and fifteen minutes later, they watched Calley and Devey appear over the rise, pushing the now-laden cart.

"Hey. Johnny, this should be a snap. We come back here next Thursday, same time, same station, and when they leave, we move in and make the snatch," said Louis.

"Yeah, we'll drive her out to the gas well, work her over a little, and convince her to talk. She don't say nuthin', you can waste her right there. A little digging, a little covering a quick skedaddle, and we're off to catch a plane from Benedum. We'll be back in civilization before dark. All neat and tidy, no muss, no fuss, just like the boss wants it."

"What about the two shoppers?" said Louis. "What are they gonna' do when they come back and report Lenya missing?"

"Louis, you worry too much. By the time they get anyone interested enough to go looking for her, she'll be long dead, and we'll be long gone. Probably go to one of those resorts in the Bahamas or in South America. We'll have lotsa' cash so we can lay back, take in the nude beaches, and live the good life for a while," Johnny assured him.

Chapter 46

There was a clattering clash of crockery and metal pans that came from the kitchen in Lenya's doublewide.

"Damn!" cried Devey, "I dropped the peanut butter again."

"Did it break?" asked Lenya.

"I think so. The jar's cracked, but it didn't make a mess. I'll pick some up when we go to the store."

"If it's something we can't do without, I'll go to the neighbors and borrow some," said Lenya.

"Never mind. There's no rush on that one. Calley's the only one who eats that crap anyway. It'll wait for our regular shopping trip, I'll pick some up then."

"I'm going over to Frank's place to visit with them and Sam Bowler tomorrow. They want a fourth for a card game, and I promised I'd play. We're going to play in the morning, and I'll have a quick bite with them, so you needn't fix anything for me. I should get back around the same time as you two, shortly after noon."

"Don't hurry back on account of us," said Calley. "We can wait lunch if you want."

"A couple of hours of cards with those people is about all I can stand. I'll eat a quick bite and duck out, even if I have to fake a headache," Lenya said.

Once again, Johnny and Louis were crouched in the tree line not far from Lenya's place. They had arrived late and fully expected to see the couple who lived with Lenya emerge from the trailer at any second. Moments passed as bugs bedeviled Louis who was impatiently swatting at them.

"How's come they's after my ass? They don't bother you at all," Louis complained.

"It's that nasty after-shave you use. You think that shit smells sexy? Well, it is to those bugs, they just want a piece of your fat ass, that's all. You got 'em all stirred up for romance."

The morning sun was now hotter than it should have been and Louis was wiping with his handkerchief. He mopped a while, then swatted and then bitched.

"I'll bet we're sittin' in poison ivy," Louis complained.

"You even know what it looks like?" asked Johnny.

"No. You?"

"Nope. Don't worry, you won't know until tomorrow. It don't break out right away, but tomorrow you'll have big blisters and welts, if it's poison ivy."

"Screw you, you're just jackin' me off."

"You're the one who—wait. There they are. They're coming out," Johnny interrupted himself.

"You see anything of the little woman?" asked Louis, conscientiously avoiding the "M" word.

"Nope, she might still be inside, still asleep, or putting her clothes on. We'll wait about fifteen minutes to give the couple a chance to get clear and give her a chance to get herself decent, then I'll try the front door. That guy might have left it unlocked. You try the back door and, if either is open, we'll meet in front and go in together. If we don't find an unlocked door, after we meet, I'll just pick the front lock. And we'll sneak in."

Johnny explained, once again, they didn't want to announce the fact they were there. He wanted to catch the woman entirely by surprise and whisk her quickly into the car before she could react.

"Just stay back and let the brains of this outfit go to work," he said to Louis.

"Hey, you be the boss. I give up thinking about things when I'm with you."

Johnny advanced toward the front door and Louis headed for the back. After a few minutes the men met toward the front of the trailer.

"Hey, Johnny," Louis began.

"Hold it down," Johnny whispered. "You don't have to tell the neighborhood we're here."

Johnny told his partner that the front door was locked and it looked like they'd have to jimmy a window or pick the lock.

"Naw," said Louis, "the back door was unlocked. Well, not really, but it had a gap big enough to get a card on the bolt. Anyway, it's unlocked now."

"You didn't make a bunch of noise, did you?"

"Quiet as a little mouse."

Together they moved to the back door and quietly entered the mobile home. It was so quiet they could hear the ticking of a clock somewhere down the hallway. They moved farther to the rear of the home where they suspected the bedrooms were.

At the rear there was a large master bedroom with furnishings and clothing that revealed it was Lenya's quarters. They poked around for a few moments, eased open the bathroom, and looked through the closets. There was no sign of the diminutive woman.

"Must be up front," Johnny whispered, motioning Louis to move and follow him up the hallway.

Both men jumped at the sudden clang and whoosh as the air conditioner noisily kicked in. The noise prompted Louis to pull out his Ruger and check to make sure the safety was on.

As they passed through the living room Louis peered behind the sofa. Finding nothing there, they moved past the kitchen and passed by a larger bathroom off the hallway. At the farthest end of the home there was a guest bedroom that belonged to the couple who had gone shopping. It proved to be empty as well.

"Nobody here," said Johnny half-heartedly.

"Wanna' ransack the place?" asked Louis with a smile.

"Yeah, and about the time we're half done, the couple will wander back in."

"What we gonna' do?"

"Lock the back door and fix it so it won't open. We want to make sure no one comes in that way," instructed Johnny. "Then we pull up a couple of chairs and wait to see who comes home first. If it's the little gal, we snatch her and that's that. If it's the couple, we can waste them right here, then wait and snatch her later."

"Couldn't we just tie 'em up and snatch the little woman?" asked Louis.

"Dead people don't make for problems. We leave them alive they become a liability. We don't need any liabilities. I don't like having to wack a couple more people, particularly after what the boss said, but I don't like taking chances either. Let's just hang back and see what develops. Maybe we're getting all worried for nothing.

"Go get in a chair in the living room near the front door. And don't go takin' a nap neither."

"The guy at the market seemed a lot more friendly than the one who was there before. You don't suppose they fired the other one?" suggested Calley.

"I seriously doubt if they ever fire anyone out here. Too hard to find replacements, I'll bet," said Devey.

"You suppose Lenya is back from Frank and Gitte's yet?" Calley asked.

"I doubt it. She said she'd stay for lunch, then leave. I figure she'll hit the door around 12:30 or so. It's 11:45 now. We can make it back to the trailer and eat lunch before she arrives.

"Maybe we could all go for a walk somewhere after lunch, like we did the other day. That was nice, and we might even drop in on some of the other folks we haven't met," Devey offered.

"We'd better be heading back then. I'd hate to eat in front of Lenya, even though she's already had her lunch."

They both waved at the gatekeeper as they passed through. He didn't speak, but vigorously waved and smiled as they went by.

Calley was panting as he pushed the cart up the drive toward the deck. He scanned the yard and trailer for signs of life and finding none, he said, "Don't look like she's back yet. Drapes are still drawn and no lights are on."

"Good," said Devey as they approached the house. "We have some time to put the groceries away and straighten things up."

Calley reached into his pocket for the keys while Devey unloaded the contents of the cart onto the deck. It was just a few steps to the door, so Calley picked up a plastic bag of jars of pickles and olives so he wouldn't have to make an extra trip for them. He looped one hand through the bag's handles and

with the other managed the keys. He turned the lock still holding the bag.

When the door opened, Calley was facing Louis, who was
sitting in an easy chair holding his .22 pointed at Calley's head.
Without much time to think about what he was doing, Calley,
in a reflex action, swung the bag at the fat man's head.

Louis went backward, chair and all, landing on his back
with a loud moan. His pistol skittered along the tiled entrance-
way, silently ending up on the living room carpet.

A surprised Johnny Stampanato walked into the room from
the bathroom. His only weapon was his icepick that was taped
to his leg. Assessing the situation, he immediately made a dive
for the pistol just as Calley made a similar decision that left the
two of them wrestling and scrabbling for advantage.

By this time Devey came through the door with another
bag. She swung at Johnny's head and kicked the gun across
the room. Johnny was knocked senseless long enough for
Devey to grab the icepick that was now exposed on Johnny's
leg. Calley rolled over and made a move for the gun as Johnny
who was returning to consciousness, made a move for the gun
himself. Frantically Devey blindly lashed out at Johnny's head
with the icepick. The point made an entry wound just under his
right eyelid and, in her horror and haste, drove it deep into his
brain, then made the wound worse by trying to withdraw the
weapon.

Johnny screamed and tried to get to his feet when Devey
struck again, this time in his neck. She left the handle of the
pick protruding and grabbed the sack that contained a six-pack
of soda. She swung it with all she had at his bleeding eye and
connected with a crunching thud. She continued hitting him
while Calley turned his attention to Louis.

Louis had regained what senses he had and was rushing toward Calley in an attempt to overpower him with the force of his weight. Unfortunately for Louis, Calley had recovered the .22 and fired one shot at the oncoming Louis.

According to those who make a living murdering folks, a .22 is deadly unless it fails to enter the skull. In Louis's case, that proved to be the problem.

While Devey was pounding out whatever life remained in Johnny Stampanato, Lenya had slipped into the trailer and, making a quick assessment, leaped past the melee to her bedroom to retrieve the Glock she knew was in her nightstand.

Calley was facing a now angry Louis. Shooting him in the head had just pissed him off, but now Lenya appeared on the scene as she jacked back the slide on the Glock.

Louis looked stunned. His hand reached to where Calley's bullet had creased his skull above his right eyebrow.

"Damn, that stings," he said as his eyes tried to fix themselves on what was going on in the room. His eyes focused on the barrel of the Glock, just as a round was jacked into the chamber. The next sound was one that he didn't hear—the sound of a 9mm slug being pushed down the barrel by the force of gasses produced by burning powder.

At a point right between Louis's eyes, give or take a millimeter or two, a black hole appeared as a bright red spray almost instantaneously spurted somewhere from the rear of his head.

Neither Calley nor Devey made a sound or move for what seemed to be an eternity. The next thing either of them heard was Lenya calling 911.

"Hello, my name is Lenya Klebb. I live at 8 Byrd Lane near Gibsonton, West Virginia," she said calmly, "There's been a home invasion and shots have been fired. Two men are down. Please send someone right away. I believe the two down are dead. Yes, I'll stay on the phone until someone arrives."

The ME Emergency bunch arrived too late to do Johnny and Louis any good, so they packed the bodies into plastic bags and loaded them into a waiting ambulance. The State Police, a County Sheriff, and his deputy and a constable descended on the community.

Not long after they arrived, a carload of government men drifted in and, along with them, Barry Pipare.

Statements were taken, a sort of investigation was conducted, evidence assembled, and a report was eventually written. The government men were more than willing to accept the conclusion of the report.

According to the official version, "Two men had entered the house to burglarize it. When Miss Keavy and Mr. Crowcroft interrupted them, they attempted to murder them. Whereupon, Keavy and Crowcroft defended themselves, resulting in the deaths of their two assailants.

It turned out that the two home invaders were well-known petty thieves, and both had extensive records. Once that was determined, the whole matter was shoved into the case-closed files, and it was as if the two men never existed.

Chapter 47

It was more than a month since the "home invasion" incident, and plans were in the works for a wedding. Calley proposed to Devey a couple of weeks after they had once again settled into their normal Gibtown routine. Calley had been offered a job mowing the commons in Gibtown proper, and Devey was doing a land-office business as a masseuse and was making house calls for a handsome price.

They decided to have the wedding ceremony on the deck and then move to the back yard for a giant reception and barbecue. Lenya said she would supply the wood for the fire from the remains of the tree her husband was chopping when he passed on.

"We'll put the past behind us and give everything a new beginning," she said. "We've got a lot of bad shit to put behind us."

"You can say that again," said Devey.

Devey and Calley planned a trip back to Dillweed for a visit to Calley's homeplace before the wedding. He wanted to put everything to rest and begin anew. He felt that he could do that with one last look back.

"I know, I know what Thomas Wolfe had to say on the subject," he told Devey. "I know it'll be nothing like it was when I left, but I have to see it and bury the past. I have ghosts to put away and demons to bury."

Devey didn't react to Calley's plan with much enthusiasm or negativity; she just went along. Fortunately for her, the past faded quickly with the death of Aunt Sis and the subsequent passing of her father. Aside from a cousin or two and some best-forgotten scenery, her home was no longer in Madison. Her heart was now, for better or worse, embedded in Gibtown.

"I hate to go off leaving Lenya alone. She may have gotten rid of a couple of threats, but I don't know if the danger will ever be gone," she said to Calley.

"She's a tough old bird, and I don't think we'll have to call on anyone to look in on her. She's been taking care of herself for all this time, and I'm sure she seen some pretty tough customers other than the thugs she helped us with. Carnies are a barbed-wire tough breed. I think she'll get by."

Lenya wasn't surprised when Barry Pipare drove up in his Crown Victoria. She knew that he was attuned to all of the happenings around and about Gibtown. In fact, she expected his arrival. She was betting he just couldn't wait until he could see her alone and pump her for information.

He got out of the car and made a show of looking around the place, then walked up on the deck and knocked. Lenya answered the door.

"Well," Lenya said, "just when you least expect visitors—"

"Hello, Lenya, can I come in?"

"This a friendly visit or a professional call?"

"I'm hoping it's both," Pipare said.

"I thought the investigation was concluded."

"Officially it is, but I still have a couple of questions I'd like answered."

"Come on in then. I'll answer anything I want, no problem."
She said with a broad smile.

Barry asked her if she had thought of anything that may
have been left out of the report. She told him there was nothing
she could come up with to add, but she would think on it.

"Come on, Lenya, you know what I mean. Where is it? And
don't play the where-is-what game with me. I'm not here to
play. I just want to know where it is," he said grimly.

"Don't have a clue what you're talking about and, if I did,
I still wouldn't have a clue, so why don't you take your little
badge and MIB glasses and hike your ass on back on down to
Charleston."

"Okay, I can see you're not interested in doing this the easy
way—yet. I was hoping you'd see this my way, but I suppose
not."

"Whatcha' gonna do, big man, put the cuffs on me?"

He reached out, grabbed a handful of her hair, and dragged
her to the sofa. He slapped her a couple of times, then once
again hard until a trickle of blood started at the corner of her
mouth.

"Don't whimper," he warned, putting a finger in her face.
"You pull a crying jag on me and I really give you a reason to
cry."

"I wouldn't give you the satisfaction you bastard moth-
erf—."

A fist and a sound like cracking bone interrupted her words.
She spit a mouthful of blood and a tooth at him as he slammed
her body into a chair.

"Now, show me where it is or I'll just wait until your friends
come back and, when they do, I'll meet them at the door with
this. He pulled out his service pistol, put it to her head and
thumbed the hammer. "I'll gag your ass and duct tape you to

that chair and make you sit and watch while I waste them. Oh, I won't take them out all at once. An arm, a leg, a gut shot, and you can watch it all, live and in living color."

Lenya sat in silence, thinking, planning, hoping, but nothing would come. It all seemed so hopeless. Maybe if she gave him the bag, he'd go away. No, he'd kill her, but maybe he'd kill her, then go away leaving her friends alone. It was a chance, and maybe she could figure some way out along the way. If she didn't do something he'd just beat her until Calley and Devey returned, then it would be too late.

"Okay, it's out there." She nodded toward the door.

"Out where?" he asked.

"Out there, under the trailer. It's in a bag, under the bathroom. You have to go outside to an access panel in the skirting. It's real tight under there, and I doubt if you can get to where it is."

She led him out to the panel, removed it, and pointed to the bulge in the insulation. "It's up there under the fiberglass," she said.

Pipare looked under the trailer through the ghostly light of the skirting which diffused the sunlight. He could see the lump in the dim glow.

"You're right, I'm not going up there after it. I'd never fit in there, but I know your ass will. I'm going to follow you in there. You reach up and get the package and hand it back to me. If you make so much as one false move I'll plug your little midget ass and leave you in there to rot."

She was pleased to notice the "M" word epithet still cut through her pain. She was still full of fight, but all she could think of now was The Mister's old stolen pistol. Her mind raced. Would it have rusted to the point it might not work or, worse yet, explode? Was it loaded? Was the ammunition so damp it wouldn't fire? Could she manage to get the gun and point the muzzle end toward him before he could stop her?

"No one would notice the smell either. All kinds of animals die under trailers all the time. You wouldn't make any more stink than a small dog," he continued his harangue.

Lenya moved the access panel to one side and crawled in on her stomach. It was only about ten feet or so to the bulge, but the insulation had sagged and within the last four feet she could barely reach out to where the bag was buried in it. She reached as far as she could and felt for the gun she knew was on top of the bag. Panic set in when she couldn't find it.

"Quit screwin' around up there," Pipare complained. "You try and pull anything, and you become a permanent part of the scenery under here."

The air was cloyingly damp and musty, and choking glass fibers drifted from where she disturbed the insulation. They both began to cough.

"You got until I count to ten, then this shit is over, you hear me?"

The gun had slipped down between the insulation and the bag. She found the grip and eased back the hammer. She put the bag on top of the gun and twisted her body to where she could see Pipare, who lay with his gun hand outstretched toward her.

"Give it to me," he said as he switched the gun to his other hand and reached for the bag.

"Here," she said, pointing the gun at his face and pulling the trigger. There was a snap and no report. The gun had misfired. Pipare tried to bring his gun hand back into position, but Lenya squeezed the double-action revolver again until another chamber was under the hammer. This time the result was a deafening bang, even for a small caliber weapon like a .22. Another

215

result was a small hole at the corner of Pipare's temple. No glancing blow this. This time the bullet entered and traveled on its gray omelet-making spin around cranial bone. The residual smell of gunpowder and Barry's lifeless form assured Lenya, it was indeed over.

She somehow dragged the lifeless body from under the claustrophobic chamber and positioned it in the garden behind the trailer. She didn't have to worry about making it look as though she were attacked. Her face was a bruised mess, her bloody mouth and her missing front tooth testimony to the story she would tell.

Pipare had arrived with rape on his mind. He had overtaken Lenya in the garden and beaten her into submission. Armed with the small gun because she was fearful of another home invasion, she was able to get the gun out and—they would believe her. After all, the only other witness was dead. Lenya was a small, defenseless, pitiful figure who had fought for her honor and won. Because Pipare was a law officer, there would be an inquest, but the finding was inevitable. A judge would never have to consider the matter.

The real reason for the attack was now safely behind the access panel, buried in insulation. In the place of the small pistol, a sturdy, fully loaded, Glock rested above the bag—just in case.

Calley and Devey soon recognized that Thomas Wolfe was right. They cut their trip short when they heard of Lenya's escape from the clutches of Barry Pipare. They had their marriage license and were prepared to hold the ceremony within the week, but now it seemed other things were far more important. Neither would have admitted how important the welfare of one tiny ex-carny had become to both of them.

Chapter 48

Early autumn was in the still warm West Virginia air. The broomsage and grasses in the fields turned red and brown, soon to be joined by crimson maples and dark oaks. Green would only survive in the mountain laurels and other evergreens that broke the rule of Appalachian autumn.

There were two times of the year Lenya preferred. She liked fall, all dressed up in multi-colored finery, and spring, when everything was new again. Winter was cold, and cold now hurt her tiny body. Summer was too much like Florida, and she had little use for it.

A coming cold front was lodged somewhere in Canada, northwest of Ohio, and it pushed the warmer air into the foothills. It was the last semblance of warm weather before flakes of snow would decorate the broomsage of the field. Soon the part of Sam Bowler's corn rejected by the crows would be harvested.

The yard behind the house was festively dressed and had been turned into a miniature midway. Carnival and carousel music blared from loudspeakers, and from time to time, a former talker would try out his never-lost-never-forgotten spiel on the crowd.

Although there were few kids to enjoy them, Devey had rented a blow-up slide, a blow-up trampoline, and a small carousel. There was no Ten in One, but some neighbors set up makeshift versions of the joints they used to run on the lot. All were gaffed hanky panks, so there were only winners. No one noticed the prizes were slum, but no one really cared.

This was "The Reception." The chaplain who usually conducted services in the clubhouse at Gibsonton conducted the ceremony earlier in the day. He had held forth on the front deck where a small party gathered as the couple exchanged vows.

The "bridal gown" was a faded pair of jeans and a Rolling Stones, tongue-protruding—logo T-shirt. She wore a train bedecked with fall flowers that looked as if it used to be a lace kitchen curtain. The groom's tux was a cut off sweatshirt and cargo pants.

Frank Lebeau, an ex-carny who ran a hootchie-kootch joint, stood in as best man. He was attired in the best red satin, sequined outfit he owned. His toreador pants looked as if they would split and expose his skinny butt at any second. As would be expected, the only one who was really dressed for the occasion was the bridesmaid, Lenya Klebb.

When the party retired to the reception area, Calley took Devey by the hand and walked her to the tiny carousel.

"Once around on the chump twister?" he asked.

"Once around," she replied, "and make sure it's going in the right direction."

They rode, played, laughed, and giggled. The evening dusk faded into darkness and wood was added to the former barbecue fire where people gathered to ward off the evening chill. As they crowded around the fire, someone near the edge yelled, "Toast! A toast to the bride and groom."

Lenya stood from a lawn chair and said in her best Husqvarna voice, "Not just yet! We have some announcements and a brief ceremony first. I don't know how this custom got started, but in my family, when someone got married, they would take one of their old, prized possessions and burn it in front of the congregation. I know, I know, y'all ain't much of a congregation, but you'll have to do. This is to symbolize a casting off of the old and a whole new fresh beginning."

The fire blazed anew when someone added a log. Flames licked into the night sky and illuminated a pole standing just over the rise behind the trailer. Behind the broken pole, stars blinked and a harvest moon was on the rise.

Calley stepped forward to the fire and reached under his shirt collar. There he retrieved a bright red amulet that had been hanging from a string around his neck—no, not an amulet. It was a whistle. In the same motion and with no explanation to anyone, he cast it like some Voodoo priest into the fire. It lay there for a moment, and it must have been steam escaping from a burning branch, but Calley could have sworn he heard a last failing gasp from the dying useless thing.

Next Devey approached the fire. Under her arm she was carrying what appeared to be no more than a bunch of old rags and yarn. No words, no comment, only the brief trickle of a tear and Missy Anne was gone.

"I have something, too," announced Lenya. "I have it right here."

She held aloft a dull red book. "I know most of you don't

know what this is. But there are some of you from over in Gib-town that know. You know who you are—I know who you are. I want you to see it one last time and tell all your friends about this night."

Murmurs arose from the rear of the crowd.

"This has more misery attached to it than any of us will ever know. It's been around for nearly a half century and now—" She fanned the pages out so it would burn quickly and threw it into the fire. "Now it's gone for good. Take note of that, you who know what it is."

Strangely, for reasons known only to each individual, most of those in the assembly applauded, none more enthusiastically than the bride and groom.

"Leave it," said Lenya to Devey. "It's your day. Leave all that mess and those dishes sit until tomorrow. Maybe we'll get a maid service to come in next week and hose this place out. If you're as tired as I am, I know you won't feel like lifting a finger for a week."

"That's an easy one for me. I'm pooped," Devey replied as both flopped into easy chairs.

Calley was on the couch with his hands behind his head. He appeared to be totally relaxed.

"Lenya, I've never seen anyone stand as tall as you did this evening. You did us proud. Are you absolutely sure that was the red book you burned tonight?" he mused as almost a throwaway idea.

"What?" Lenya tried to sound incredulous. "I'm shocked. Do you think a poor little old widowed, ex-carny midget would pull the old switcheroo?"

Daniel I. Morris
...is a retired college professor and newspaper publisher. He lives with his wife Barbara in Southwestern Pennslyvania and they winter in Central Florida.

www.ingramcontent.com/pod-product-compliance
Lightning Source LLC
Chambersburg PA
CBHW070112260626
47160CB00004B/1436